THE PRICE OF DREAMS

Faith & Fortune 3

TONI SHILOH

Toni Shiloh

Scripture taken from the New King James Version®. Copyright © 1982 by Thomas Nelson. Used by permission. All rights reserved.

Edited by Katie Donovan.

Cover design by Toni Shiloh.

Cover art photos © Shutterstock.com/Gorbash Varvara used by permission.

Published in the United States of America by Toni Shiloh.

www.ToniShiloh.com

The Price of Dreams is a work of fiction. Names, characters, places, and incidents are either products of the author's imagination or used fictitiously. All characters are fictional, and any similarity to people living or dead is purely coincidental.

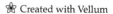 Created with Vellum

DEDICATION

To the Author and Finisher of my faith.

1

I EXHALED AND MOVED INTO A *FOUETTÉ EN TOURNANT EN dehors*. Using my right leg to extend and come back in at a triangle, I thrust my body around in a full turn. Muscle memory immediately propelled my legs through a *glissade* and into fourth position before making the transition into a *grand jeté*. I leapt into the air, exhilarating in the freedom of the movement as the music's crescendo stirred the scene to one of joy and exultation.

My partner moved to my side and swooped me into a fish dive, my face dangerously close to the floor. No panic—only trust resided, because we'd done this sequence over and over and over, each time perfecting the movements. The constant training I'd put my muscles and mind through commanded my limbs, every inch of me presented to the audience with precision.

Ballet was the ultimate visual art, and I was completely aware that my physical form embodied the passion and story the choreographers and musicians wanted to tell, letting the audience in on the secrets of love and heartache, overcoming and triumphant happiness.

I bent at the waist, my right knee kneeling on the stage in

a *révérence*, or curtsy, as the music came to an end. The crowd rose to their feet with a roar of applause. But the ovation wasn't meant for me. Not for me alone, anyway. It took more than one person to pull off a performance. Every production required a massive team effort to look seamless and fluid.

I blinked as the memory faded and reality set in.

I, Octavia Ricci, am a principal ballerina for the City Ballet Company. Or rather, I *was*. Now the only dances I could perform were those in my memory. Last month, I'd received the call informing me that another ballerina would take my starring position as principal ballerina for the performances my body could no longer execute. One attack from a stalker and my knee had failed me. Not *my* stalker, but my best friend's, Tori Bell.

Wait, she's Tori Fox now.

Anyhow, the assault left me with a ruptured ligament in my knee and a note of warning from the doctor that I may never dance again.

Never dance again?

Those words made no sense. I couldn't comprehend them, though I lay here in a hospital bed recovering from anterior cruciate ligament (ACL) reconstruction surgery. The doctor had given me three options prior to cutting me open. Number one: they could use a donor graft, taking an ACL from a deceased individual and grafting the tissues into my body.

I shuddered at the thought every time it sprang to mind. *Ew!* Although the easiest option, it wouldn't guarantee my return to the dance I loved so much.

Option two had been to graft tissue from my patella. This choice made me less queasy. However, I would have been left with a partial knee cap. Kind of needed that for stability in dancing. The last route proved to be the most difficult and came with the longest recovery time. Yet picking this choice gave me the best chance of returning to ballet at the same level I had performed before. After gaining my consent, the surgeon had taken part of my hamstring to reconstruct a new ACL.

Now my left leg burned with pain.

I shifted in the hospital bed and moaned, then studied the whiteboard in my room where the nurse had kindly written the times I was scheduled to receive another dose of pain medication. The initial narcotics had torn my stomach apart, leaving me hovering over a pink plastic container and needing new sheets, since I'd missed the bowl the first time my insides revolted.

Now I was relegated to nonnarcotic pain medication and anti-inflammatories, alternating between the two to keep my pain under control. I pressed the nurse icon on my remote and waited for someone at the station to respond. A voice spoke through the room intercom system and told me my nurse would be right in.

I sighed. Hopefully, the doctor would let me go home tomorrow. For some reason, he wanted me to stay the night for observation. Which, granted, if he hadn't made the order, I never would have realized the awful affect the narcotic drugs had on my body.

Two taps rapped on the door and then it swung open. "Afternoon, Ms. Ricci. Time for some pain meds?" the nurse asked.

"Please, Dianne." I smiled at the petite RN. She was a sweetheart and didn't deserve any bad attitude from me. It was a struggle to remember my manners through the haze of pain though.

She handed me a measuring cup with two tablets in it and passed the hospital mug full of water. "Here you go, sweetie." She pushed her glasses up the bridge of her nose.

"Thank you." I downed the meds and handed her the empty cup and water.

"Very good. I looked at your chart, and your physical therapist will be in soon."

I bit back a groan. Wasn't it bad enough I'd already been tortured by him prior to surgery? Apparently having PT before surgery was supposed to help me heal faster afterward. All I knew was it was torturous, and now that I'd had the surgery, I expected the level of pain and annoyance to increase exponentially.

"All right."

"Rest until he comes, dear."

"Okay." I offered a smile, even though I knew resting would be impossible.

I hadn't slept well with all the comings and goings. You'd think the meds would've helped, but the pain in my leg and the thought of never dancing again kept me from sleeping soundly. In fact, I hadn't slept a full eight hours since the attack. But I would squeeze my eyes shut and try.

In the past, I would've sung a gospel or Christian song to lull myself to sleep, but since my ACL rupture, God had been quiet. Had left me out in the cold, alone, without a word from Him. The Bible said that He would never forsake us, but the silence, the empty void that greeted me when I called out to Him, said otherwise.

Didn't it?

"Therapy time."

I blinked at the voice that intruded on my thoughts. Had it been a half hour already? I glanced at the clock and then at my physical therapist—Dr. Noah Wright.

"Good afternoon, Octavia." His gaze assessed me then shifted away.

Noah always seemed uncomfortable saying my name, which was odd, because he'd asked that I use his instead of calling him Dr. Wright. Maybe being on a first name basis with me was too personable for him? Did other clients insist on being called by their first name? I wasn't a formal person, so it made no sense to be referred to as Ms. Ricci. Or maybe that was my way of distancing myself from my father.

I stared at the green-eyed doctor. His brown hair was always mussed in multiple directions. Was he one of those men who ran his fingers through his hair when stressed, or did he simply refuse to use a brush?

But that wasn't what gave me pause every time he came around. It was his quiet demeanor that promised he'd listen to every word you had to say. Those penetrating eyes that seemed to see deep into my soul to the pain I kept stuffing down.

"Good afternoon, Noah." My voice was quiet, hesitant. Because, truthfully, I was still trying to work out this strange dynamic between us. Sure, he was personable and friendly at times, but I always got the sense he was holding back. And I really wanted to know why.

Maybe my fame threw him off. Ever since I'd received the position of principal ballerina, I'd been plastered all over the newsstands. Though, not as much as my best friends, Tori and Holiday. For one, Tori was a supermodel, recently married, and a kidnapping survivor. Holiday was a platinum-recording pop singer engaged to Tori's brother, who also happened to be a Pulitzer Prize-winning photographer.

Next to them, my notoriety seemed tame. But being one of two African American principal ballerinas in America—formerly, now—gave me some limelight next to Misty Copeland, the other African American principal. Being the daughter of winemaker Donovan Ricci put me in other elite circles—because everyone wanted a bottle of Ricci Winery's finest.

Nah. Why would an educated doctor, a specialist in sports injuries, be intimidated by me? I scoffed under my breath. "What's the plan today, Doc?"

He pierced me with his eyes.

I corrected myself. "Noah."

"I actually just want to do some light stretching. We don't

want your leg to tense or tighten up more." He smiled at me. He always seemed more self-assured when talking medicine.

I had to admit, he was good looking for a white guy. I'd never dated a Caucasian before. Not because I hated that part of myself, but because the world saw me as Black, and I knew from my parents' own experience that interracial relationships only caused headaches.

Not that I'd dated a lot anyway. I'd been too involved with ballet to give my love to any man, white or Black.

"We need to give your leg and knee good feedback." Noah's soft voice interrupted my musings. "I'll do a light massage so your nerve receptors will relax some and give your body the message everything will be okay."

I met his gaze, trying to focus on his words and ignore the pain and random thoughts floating in my head. "Okay."

He pushed back the blanket, keeping my right leg underneath for a veil of modesty and propriety. I looked down at my other leg wrapped in gauze.

"Does it hurt?"

"Yes."

He nodded and placed his hands behind my calf. "How's this?"

"No pain there."

"Good. You relax and let me just slowly work your leg up."

I nodded and closed my eyes, inhaling and exhaling slow and steady breaths. The fluidity of ballet had introduced me to controlled breathing a long time ago. The more I could relax, the better the stretch Noah would be able to give my left leg.

"Octavia?"

"Yes?" I cracked an eyelid at the cautious tone in his voice and found Noah staring at me. Was something wrong? Both of my eyes sprang open.

"What do you want out of your therapy sessions?"

Huh? He'd already asked me this when we first met in October, hadn't he? "I want to dance again. You know this."

A half smile curved his lips. "I know, but at what level? Recreational? Professional? Do you want me to take it easy on you or push you, knowing I'll stop before your body reaches its limits?"

My thigh tensed as he hit a painful area.

"Relax," he instructed as he moved my leg up, extending my fiery hamstring.

I purposely blew out a breath, my brow furrowing. "I need to be a principal ballerina again. I do *not* need coddling, *Dr.* Wright."

His puppy-dog eyes met mine then bounced away. "Ouch. I didn't mean to tick you off." He held my leg steady, sustaining the stretch. "I want to know your goals so that I can ensure we meet them."

Oh. I bit my lip, studying him. "I apologize."

He averted his eyes and lowered my leg back down. "How does it feel?"

I did a mental body assessment, much like the ones I'd do after practicing or performing. "It hurts less."

"Good. Positive feedback will help in your recovery, but we will push you so you can get back to center stage." He held out his hand, finally meeting my gaze. "Deal?"

I slipped my hand in his, ignoring the way my heart seemed to sigh at the warmth of his touch.

Shaking his hand always produced this effect.

And I always ignored it. "Deal."

2

I HELD IN A WINCE AS FOX CARRIED ME UP TO THE FIFTH FLOOR, where my room waited. Dr. Wright didn't want me to use the stairs yet, but Holiday, Tori, and I lived in a five-story town-house in Manhattan. And, of course, my personal living space was on the top floor. The level encompassed my bedroom suite and ballet studio. The only thing higher than my floor was the rooftop with its attached guest room.

Thankfully, Tori's husband was strong and could manage my five-foot-three petite frame up the stairs with ease. Why had we never considered putting in an elevator? Not like we couldn't afford the expense. All of us had our own money and the trusts our parents had set us up with when we turned eighteen. Poor, we were not.

That's an understatement, Tavi.

I shifted my thoughts, hoping to think *light as a feather* and ease Fox's burden.

"You don't have to hold your breath. I think you weigh less than my niece."

Tori chuckled behind him. They seemed to be attached at the hip since their nuptials two weeks ago.

I exhaled then inhaled. "How was your honeymoon?" I

asked. They had spent time in the Poconos, leaving their cell phones behind.

"Perfect," Tori purred.

Fox avoided my gaze. "It was good."

"Such a man." Tori snorted.

"More like gentleman," Fox retorted.

"Good to see your bickering survived the honeymoon." I shook my head. Sparks had been flying between Fox and Tori since the day her father had hired him as her bodyguard.

Somehow, between a fake engagement to lure her stalker out, injuries—bullet wounds included—and a kidnapping, they'd managed to fall in love. All the while, they battled with words like a seasoned married couple. It was cute if you liked sappy happily-ever-afters.

Okay, honestly, I loved the romance of it all. Their November wedding had been stunning in its fall glory. I just didn't know how much romance a person could actually expect in the everyday real world. Fairy tales were called *tales* for a reason, you know?

Tori rushed ahead of Fox as we stepped onto the fifth-floor landing. She headed to the left to open my bedroom door.

"Should I put you on your bed, Ms. Ricci? I mean, Tavia." Fox was having a hard time remembering we were honorary in-laws. I wasn't related to Tori, but she was like a sister in better ways than biology, so it counted.

"Yes, please." I smiled as he settled me onto the bed. The room was filled with flowers, balloons, stuffed animals, and cards from my friends and colleagues at the ballet company. They hadn't forgotten me.

"Need anything?" Fox asked.

"No, thank you. I appreciate you carrying me, and I promise you won't have to do that often."

Tori frowned, lines furrowing her brow and concern darkening her blue-green eyes to a deep pine-green. "Are you sure we shouldn't hire someone to see to you? A day nurse?"

"You already supplied me with a mini fridge of snacks." I stared at the appliance next to my dresser.

"I know, but still."

"I'll be fine, Tor. Breathe." Shouldn't I be the one tied up in knots?

Okay, so I was, but Tori didn't know just how much. Couldn't. I needed her to believe I was okay so she could go live her married life and enjoy her new status as Mrs. Marcel Fox.

She blew out a breath. "Fine. When's your hot doctor coming again?"

"Excuse me?" Fox arched an eyebrow.

"Oh, you have nothing to worry about." She wrapped her arms around him and kissed his lips.

"*Per amor del cielo!* You're in *my* bedroom." Though my exclamation came out in Italian and not English, the tone of my voice must have given a clue to my level of irritation.

Tori pulled away, her light brown cheeks turning rosy. "Sorry. Got distracted by this walking chocolate bar."

I hid a giggle as Fox shoved his hands in his pockets and turned his gaze toward the ceiling. He was classically tall, dark, and handsome, skin the darkest of brown without a blemish in sight. But I didn't want her to know how adorable I found them. "Gag, Tor. Please, go enjoy your newlywedded bliss somewhere else."

"Sorry, Tavia," Fox's low voice rumbled as he guided Tori out of my room.

The door clicked shut, and silence echoed off the walls. All alone once again.

My head fell back against the plush headboard as I let go of my *I'm okay* attitude. In truth, I was *not* happy. I couldn't be until the doctor proclaimed me a hundred percent healed and I was back on the stage. Until then, I was stuck in some weird limbo state where I fluctuated between full-on despair and a place where I was able to laugh and joke with my girlfriends.

Not that they were around much anymore. Holiday was always with Emmett. They'd gotten engaged a few months ago and were planning a summer wedding after Holiday's tour finished. She devoted every single free moment to Emmett except for the scheduled dates we girls had—our standing Sunday brunch and a few spa days here and there.

They allowed us to catch up on each other's lives, since we rarely passed each other in this monstrosity of a house. But now that I was stuck up here, would I be able to keep our plans? I didn't want to battle five floors of stairs just to go out in public and be on display with a knee brace. I could see the headlines now. *Former principal ballerina, Octavia Ricci, well enough to do brunch, but will she return to the stage?*

No, thank you.

The back of my eyelids stung with tiny pricks of heat. The warmth spread, and the first tear spilled. Since I'd gotten the diagnosis of a ruptured ACL, I couldn't seem to stop crying.

Wait, not true. I could put on a brave face when everyone else was around asking me how I was doing. I could let a little of the hurt out so they didn't feel excluded. But my friends hadn't seen me cry in years. I could *not* cry in front of them now.

Besides, Tori already felt bad enough that her stalker had cost me my career. I couldn't share how disheartened I really was. Not when there was so much else going on in the world that was worse than my reconstructed ACL. I had access to top surgeons. A physical therapist that came to my house. I literally lacked nothing.

Tears seemed the ultimate decline into a pity party, so I saved them for when I was truly alone and could only suffer the condemnation from myself. I swiped at the ones spilling down my cheeks, trying to keep my sobs quiet. Not that I really had to. No one else lived on this floor, so I didn't have to worry about sound traveling. But still, keeping silent seemed to be the best thing to do.

"Where are You, Lord?" I whispered. "Why can I not feel Your presence?"

Silence filled my ears, and the distance loomed before me. God had seen me through so much. Why had He chosen now to be silent? Didn't He know how desperately I needed a word of comfort?

I grabbed my cell off the nightstand and scrolled through my contacts. Who could I call to bring a little light into my world? *Mom* stared back at me in the M section of my list. I'd told her what had happened, and she'd offered to come and take care of me, but I'd said no.

Maybe I shouldn't have. She always brought a certain chaos with her, though not necessarily in a bad way. Still, she was my mom, and I loved her. Before I could change my mind, I pressed the telephone icon.

"Tavi, sweetheart, how are you?"

I pressed my cheek against my cell, wishing it were her hand. "Hi, Mom."

"Are you all right? Did the surgery go as you expected? Tori texted that you're home."

"I am. In my room looking around."

"And climbing the walls with boredom?"

I grinned. "Not yet. I just got here."

"Ha!" Her hearty laugh filled my ears and brought a rush of memories. It had been us two against the world. My parents had divorced a year after my birth, though their relationship remained tumultuous every time they had to make parental decisions. Per the divorce, my father got me in the summers, and that was the only time I saw him.

My mom had taken me to every ballet practice. Every recital. Sat in the front row of every performance until I'd turned eighteen. Then she'd decided to live her own life. Her words, not mine.

"Are you in a lot of pain?"

Tears blurred my vision once more, but I refused to let them fall. "I am. But I'm ignoring it."

"Good. You're a strong Black woman and can endure anything that's thrown your way."

Could I? I bit my lip. "Mom, did you still want to come?"

"If you need me, I'll be there in a heartbeat."

I chuckled. "I don't think you'll get here that fast."

"Ha. You obviously don't know me that well. Are you decent?"

"What kind of question is that?" I stared at the phone, wondering what she was up to.

"Eh, it doesn't matter. Not like I haven't seen you in your birthday suit. I did bring you into this world."

"Mom, *what* are you talking about?"

"Tavi, hang up the phone."

My head swiveled to my doorway as the words echoed through the phone and in my room. My mom stood at the foot of my bed, blue tote handbag hanging from her wrist. Her black hair was pulled back into a slick bun—the same hairstyle she'd been wearing since I started attending ballet lessons. Her warm brown face stared into mine. We had the same pointed chin, but my face was slender and hers full to match her figure.

"Mom…"

"You know I'm always here for you." She rounded the bed as she dropped her bag. Then she was by my side and wrapping her arms around me.

I placed my head on her buxom chest and sighed, feeling much younger than my twenty-six years. Her hand rubbed soothing circles on my back. "Just rest now. Mom's going to make it all better."

Tears dripped from my face, and for once, I believed she could simply kiss my hurts away. "Thank you for coming."

"Always, Tavi. Always."

3

Dr. Noah Wright was back.

I placed my full weight on my good leg as I left my bedroom using the crutches they'd given me at the hospital. Slowly, I crossed the hall and hobbled into my studio. A month ago, Noah had turned the space into a temporary physical therapy room. He'd brought in an exam table and some equipment I could use to help the healing process and build my strength back up.

Still, my heart cracked as my fingers squeezed around the grip of the crutch instead of my barre, which now served as nothing more than a rack for my workout towel. My hunched over form mocked from my reflection, and memories of standing tall and elegant in fifth position, my feet turned out so that my left heel touched the toe of my right foot, ripped at my heart.

I didn't feel like I had four weeks of therapy under my belt. Not with the way my knee burned and quads quaked. I was back to day one. Leg still wrapped in surgical gauze—per doctor's orders—and getting ready to do basic stretches. Noah had asked my mom to come to the end of my session today so he could show her the exercises she could help me with to promote quicker healing. For now, she was exploring the library and probably looking for a good streaming show to pass the time.

My fervent prayer was that Noah could really get me back to dancing at a performing level before the company forgot about me and filled their troupe with younger, more athletic dancers. Ones who hadn't suffered career-threatening injuries. I swallowed against the lump in my throat, feeling the threat of tears once more, and drew in a steadying breath as I sat on the exam table.

Noah looked up from the bench where he'd spread towels, measuring equipment, resistance bands, and massage cream. "You're walking awfully slow. Are you in a lot of pain, Octavia?"

I bit my lip and studied him. Calm exuded from him, but his green eyes were steeped in concern. "I'm okay."

"Do you hurt?"

I shrugged.

He sighed.

I bit back a smile. "I'm not trying to be difficult. I can't stomach the narcotics. They make me nauseous, but the Motrin and Tylenol aren't doing the trick either."

"Are you icing your leg? Elevating it?"

"Yes, Doctor—"

He arched an eyebrow.

"Noah." I tilted my head. "You can't be irate that I still want to call you Doctor. That's what you are. Besides, I get the feeling you're not entirely comfortable being on a first name basis."

His face reddened, and his ears flamed bright.

How adorable!

I batted the thought aside. He was my doctor. I couldn't let my curiosity to know him better make me bridge the gap between the truth—patient-doctor relationship only.

"Maybe I think it's such a big name for someone so...small."

"Are you calling me short, Noah?" I held back the note of humor, aiming for seriousness even though I was teasing.

His Adam's apple bobbed. "Uh, no. Um, petite?"

I giggled at his discomfort, covering my mouth and hating the tinkle of my laugh. It was as "petite" as my frame, and people often said the sound reminded them of a teenager. I'd been hoping it would age as I did, but so far, nothing. Still stuck being labeled a giggler.

Noah smiled. "You're teasing."

"Just a bit."

He shook his head, running his hand through his brown hair. Now his fine locks were even messier, giving him an absent-minded professor look.

Doctor. Patient. Only. I cleared my throat. "What's on the agenda for today?"

"Just stretches. We won't do much until those stitches come out."

"Can I do the stretches on my own?"

"I'd rather you didn't." Confidence surged in his voice as he continued. "I don't want you extending farther in the stretch than you should. You could do damage to your hamstring or your knee. I'll show your mom a few so she can ensure they're done properly and can help you on the days I don't come by."

My stomach dropped. "I thought we'd be doing more extensive therapy than simple stretching."

"Octavia, I've got your back." His voice was steady, determined.

"Thank you," I whispered.

"You're in pain and your body is extra tense. Right now, the best thing for you is stretching and positive feedback so your muscles don't tense up further. Remember?"

I nodded.

"Good. Please lie down."

I lay back, and he immediately went to work manipulating my leg to stretch out my hamstring. I tried to ignore the feel of his hands through my pant leg. Not like he was being untoward or improper. I just couldn't keep my mind from focusing on the pressure of his fingers. The warmth of his touch seeping through the layers of fabric.

Ugh. I cleared my throat. "So how did you become a concierge doctor?" It still amazed me I could pay for a doctor to come to my home based off my own schedule.

"My parents."

"Tell me more, please."

"Well." Noah swallowed. "I knew from an early age I wanted to help people. It wasn't until high school that I figured out how to go about doing that."

"What made you choose physical therapy?"

"I broke my arm when I was fifteen."

My lips parted. "How?" I held my breath as I awaited his reply.

His face turned red, and he averted his gaze. "Uh, I was going through some things. I climbed out the window and missed my landing."

"*Mio Dio,*" I murmured. *Lord, he must have hurt terribly.*

His eyebrows rose. Guess I hadn't spoken as quietly as I'd thought.

"Did you just say something in Italian?"

"I did."

He cocked his head to the side. "Are you part Italian?"

"Yes. My father's from Tuscany." Which was how I *knew* interracial relationships didn't work. Especially ones that crossed nationalities as well. It was bad enough I had to waffle somewhere between Black and white, but add to that being American and Italian? *Headache city.*

All my summers had been spent in Tuscany with my father's *other* family.

"And your mom?"

"She's from Brooklyn."

"An American and an Italian, huh?"

"A *Black* American and Italian," I stressed. Let's throw out all the crazy at once.

Noah chuckled. "We all have our issues."

"Are you saying my biracial status is an issue?"

"What?" His eyes bulged in horror.

I bit the inside of my lip to keep from laughing and tipping him off.

His gaze narrowed. "You're teasing me again, aren't you?"

"Maybe." My lips twitched.

He lowered my leg down to the tabletop and poked me in my stomach. "Don't. Not funny."

I giggled, hating how ticklish I was. "Stop. That's not professional."

He jumped back as if I'd turned into a spider and he had arachnophobia. His ears went beet red as he looked everywhere but at me.

I sat up, stunned by the guilt penetrating my gut. "I did *not* mean it like that. I know you're professional. I was only teasing." I inhaled, my pulse pounding in my throat. "I'm sorry, Dr. Wright."

Noah squeezed his eyes shut. "No. I am." His Adam's apple went up then down. "I'll tell your mom about those exercises. Have a good day."

He grabbed his bag, stuffing his towels into it before flying out of the room.

My heart pounded as I stared down at my leg. What had just happened? Did he think I would file harassment charges or something? Heat flooded my face. He had to know I wasn't accusing him. More tears burned my eyes.

Don't cry. Enough of that already.

But it was no use. Liquid spilled onto my cheek. I had

insulted a man who'd been nothing but nice to me. I wouldn't be surprised if I never saw him again.

And that thought hit me like a ton of bricks. Harder than it should for just a patient-doctor relationship. Why was life so very, very hard?

My cell pinged and I opened the incoming text.

C: Hey, Octavia. How are you feeling?

Up for some company?

O: Hey, Celeste. I'd love some company. When were you thinking of stopping by?

C: Rehearsals are crazy, but I'll make the time. How about I stop over and bring dinner?

O: Sounds great. Thank you.

C: Of course! See you later.

Now I would have to prepare my mind to switch from agonizing over Noah's response to wondering what Celeste wanted. Could it be something as simple as her wanting to check up on me?

I hoped so.

4

Celeste showed up at my house with Chinese food and ballet company gossip.

"You'll never believe who got together," she announced after swallowing a bite of her sweet and sour chicken. Her gray eyes twinkled with mischief as her grin widened.

I chewed my Mongolian beef. "Who?"

"Eric and Yasmine."

My chopsticks halted midair. "Really?" I thought they hated each other.

The two had always argued, to the point where they'd been threatened with expulsion if they couldn't get along. Last I knew, they kept their bickering to mutterings under their breath and visual daggers.

"Yes!" Celeste's blonde hair jiggled precariously from her messy bun. "I saw them kissing in the wardrobe closet."

"Well, then, I guess there's no disputing that."

"Definitely not. Now every time one of them passes me, they're super sweet. I don't think they want anyone else finding out."

"Have you told anyone else?"

"Nope." She dabbed her mouth. "Just you. I figured a little

news from the company would help you not miss it too much."

I sighed. Miss it I did. "Thanks, Celeste."

"Sure thing." She pointed her chopsticks toward my leg. "What's the status on your knee and rehab?"

"It's going to be at least six months of physical therapy sessions before they'll have a better idea if I can return to dancing."

"Oh wow, that's a long time."

Tell me about it. Every time I thought of what could happen in ballet over a six-month period, sweat beads popped across my upper lip. Would they return my principal spot when I was cleared by the doctors, or would I have to battle for the position against someone younger and healthier?

Ballet was an art, but also a business. Dollar signs had a certain level of sway in every decision the company made. I wouldn't fault them if I lost my spot permanently. No matter how much the decision would eviscerate me.

"Does it still hurt?"

"Yes. I'm keeping it elevated." I shook my head. *Duh, Octavia.* She could see that, since I had some throw pillows stacked under my leg. "Icing it and doing the exercises and stretches that my doctor prescribed."

"That's good. We all miss you. The more you follow doctor's orders, the quicker you'll return."

"I hope so," I murmured.

Celeste placed her hand over mine. "I know so."

I stared at the contrasting colors of our skin. Hers fair, mine not. Two very different people but fast friends. We'd both joined the company as underdogs. Celeste didn't have the background I did. Having grown up poor, she hadn't started dancing until high school. But she was one of the hardest-working ballerinas I knew, hence the reason she'd earned a spot in the company in the first place.

"I get the feeling something else is bothering you."

"It's my physical therapist. I think I insulted him." I told Celeste about *the incident.* The one that made me feel like a horrible human being. I blew out a breath. "What do you think?"

"He tickled you?"

"Well, more like a poke to my belly. You know, Pillsbury style." My face was heating up, and I had the strong urge to cover my face.

A sly grin curved Celeste's mouth. "You *like* him, and he likes *you.*"

"What? No."

"Oh yes. It's why he fled like the hounds of Hell were on his heels. He was worried about being improper because he's thinking of you more than a patient."

Was it true? Could Noah be interested in me?

"I don't know. Maybe he's just very proper."

"And you? Are you too proper to date your doctor?"

I snorted, but my brain briefly entertained the thought of Noah and me. "No dating, period."

"Why not?" She tilted her head to the side. "Now that I think about it, I can't really recall you ever saying you had a date."

My cheeks heated. "I'm too busy."

"Not right now. Why not go out?"

"The crutches make it cumbersome."

"But not impossible. If the guy can't get over the crutches, then he's not a good guy in the first place."

I sighed. "Yeah, but—"

"No buts. Just do it. One date. I can set you up if you want."

"No," I shouted. I blew out a huff of air. "I'm sorry. But no thanks. I'll handle my own relationships."

"You better, or I'm opening my contact list to find you someone."

I shuddered. "It's really not necessary. I'm capable of finding someone on my own." At least, I thought I was.

I'd been on dates before, just never very many. Ballet took up too much of my time, and I wasn't willing to spend the rest of it with a guy who would probably want more than I could give. Now that I had all this free time, I had to admit I was going out of my mind slowly but surely.

"Are all the performances for *Carmen* going well?" It was one of my favorite movies, and I so wanted to dance to the music of Georges Bizet.

"Yes." Celeste bopped her head up once before stuffing her mouth with more sweet and sour chicken. "We all miss you though. And I think Jess may have a stroke if she doesn't calm down."

My ears perked up at the name of the dancer who had replaced me. "Why's that?"

"She feels so much pressure to be as good as you. I keep telling her there's a reason we have understudies and she wouldn't have gotten that spot if she wasn't good. But she's stressing hard."

I bit my lip. "Let her know I'll be praying."

Celeste shook her head. "Only you would pray for competition."

"We're all in this together. If one looks bad—"

"Yeah, yeah. Then we all do." She chuckled.

Obviously, I had said that more than once. "Well, it's true. The audience watches everyone, not just the principal."

"I know. But Jess just feels the lights on her and no one else."

"I'll text her later."

"She'd probably appreciate that."

My mind wandered, and soon Celeste broke the silence to say good night. She had an early class in the morning and needed to head off for some much-needed rest. I thanked her for the company and the food.

Before I could forget, I zipped off a text to Jess, letting her know I was thinking of her and praying for her success. Although my stomach twisted at the what ifs—what if she *was* better than me—I pressed send and ignored the doubts swirling around me.

5

"OCTAVIA, DEAR, IT'S TIME FOR YOU TO WAKE UP."

I blinked at my mom, rubbing the sleep from my eyes. "What time is it?"

"Eight o'clock."

I never slept this late. Then again, what was the point of getting up early if I couldn't do the one thing that gave my life purpose—dancing? I pulled the covers higher. "I think I'll get some more rest."

"Oh no you don't."

A draft of cold air hit me as my mom yanked back my comforter. "Your doctor will be here in an hour. You need to shower, eat, and find that sunny disposition we all love."

I squinted my eyes at her, and she rolled hers back at me.

"Don't give me that look. The shower's not for you alone." She waved a hand in front of her face. "Phew, girl. Don't let yourself go just because you can't dance right now. Strong Black women do not wallow, Tavi, dear."

"Whatever, Mom," I muttered.

She shook my arm. "Don't you *whatever* me. Get. Up."

"*Per amor del cielo.* I'm up." I shifted in the bed, careful not to jostle my leg.

Intense throbbing greeted me as I grabbed the crutch my mom offered. I gingerly swung my leg over and placed all my weight on my right foot. Standing straight, I shifted the crutches under my armpits and tottered my way to the bathroom.

Mom followed behind me. "A shower would be easiest."

"I don't have stitches anymore. I can take a bath if I want." Why was I so contrary this morning? I hated baths, and my tub was as unused as the day I moved in. I rubbed my face.

"And how do you think you'll climb in and out of your tub? It's so deep."

My lips flattened. "I'll take a shower."

"So grouchy in the morning."

"Sorry, Mother," I huffed.

"Great, now you're calling me *Mother.*" She mumbled under her breath as she turned the shower on, placing a towel where I could reach, before exiting the bathroom and heading to my dresser. "T-shirt and yoga pants again?" she called over her shoulder.

"Yes, please."

She rummaged through my drawers. "When are you getting out of this house?"

"When I don't have to climb five sets of stairs?"

"You know Fox or Emmett can carry you, right? Heck, I'm sure that cute Dr. Wright would be more than willing as well."

"Mother, please."

After our last appointment I wasn't even sure the "cute Dr. Wright"—no, just no, he was Noah—would be coming back, let alone offering to carry me down any flights of stairs. If only I'd kept my teasing thoughts to myself. If he did show, he'd probably be more guarded than ever. Then again, maybe it was all for the best. Our relationship couldn't go past patient and doctor.

My mom came back into the bathroom and placed a set of

clean clothes on the counter. "There you go. Yell if you need help."

"I won't."

"Still."

"Okay."

She winked and shut the door behind her.

I placed a shower cap on and gradually set the crutches aside and got in the shower. My thoughts plagued me as I scrubbed. My pain level. Ballet. Thoughts of God. It was like rupturing my ACL had ripped my faith apart. I turned the water off and exhaled a shaky breath then wiped my face with a towel, hoping my tears would get the message to stop annoying me with their presence. I hadn't left the house since returning home from surgery, and my face had been devoid of makeup ever since. Maybe if I put on a little foundation and a bit of lip gloss and mascara to detract from the puffiness crying had generated, I'd stop the tears altogether.

After arranging my hair in the same style as my mother's, I added diamond stud earrings to my lobes. The jewels added a touch of class to my *Bun Hair Don't Care* ballet T-shirt and black yoga pants. I grabbed the crutches and walked out of the bathroom.

The delicious aroma of bacon greeted me as I edged closer to my king-sized bed. On top of the white down comforter, a tray holding a bowl of fresh fruit, Greek yogurt, granola, and a side of turkey bacon beckoned. A glass of fresh-squeezed orange juice accompanied the setup.

"Thank you, Mom," I called out, assuming she was still somewhere on the fifth floor.

As much as I appreciated breakfast in bed, the thought of something spilling on my white comforter made me cringe. My bedroom was light and airy, and that was mostly because I'd decorated in a color palette of whites and pale pinks. White furniture, because I liked the minimalist effect of white, but subdued pink accents to add a touch of coziness—hence my lamps, the chandelier, the extra blanket on my bed, and my throw pillows were all pink.

My mother walked in. "Oh good, you're out."

"Yes, could you please move that?" I gestured toward the food, hoping she'd move the tray to the desk near the windows.

"Sure. You know, if you got a darker bedspread, you wouldn't have to worry about spills."

"Of course I would. A spill is a spill is a spill. That's why kitchens and dining rooms were invented."

"Always have something smart to say."

I sighed and sat down. "Thank you for breakfast."

"You're welcome." She looked at the small wristwatch on her arm. "You have twenty minutes."

"Yes, ma'am."

"Oh, and Tavi?"

I looked up as she paused in the doorway. "Yes?"

"Your father said to call him."

I blinked. Blinked again. "*Scusi*?" And just like that, the mention of my father reverted me back to his native tongue.

"You've been avoiding his calls. Did you really think he'd let you ignore him for much longer?"

"No," I murmured.

She blew me a kiss. "You can do it. Be a good girl and call him after your therapy session."

"Fine."

Nerves gathered as I finished my meal and stared at my cell phone clock. Any moment, the good doctor would walk back into my sanctuary as if his very presence were nothing extraordinary. He would come in, place his bag of torture tools on the table, and then make me do mundane activities like place my heel on a rolled towel and extend my knee. Sounded simple enough until you'd had someone cut pieces of your hamstring and sew them into your knee.

There had to be a way to bring back the ease that had been

developing between us before I uttered that thoughtless, albeit teasing, accusation. I hated the thought of my sessions being filled with stilted silence.

But it's for your own good, remember? Interracial relationships only bring heartache.

That's why my father had a whole new family. One complete with an Italian wife and two children who could carry the legacy of Ricci Winery into the future. My half-brother and half-sister—twins, no less—were perfect children. They were already married, even though they were only twenty-four. My brother, Don Jr., had married his high-school sweetheart at twenty-one, and Bianca had married last summer.

Don already had a son, and his wife was pregnant with baby number two. They were a reminder that I could never compete for my father's affections, so I didn't even try. I called him when he nagged my mother to nag me, and then I remained silent until the next admonishment.

I hadn't been to Italy since Bianca married. My days of staying for the summer were long over. Now only special occasions called me across the Atlantic.

The doorbell pealed through the house, and I rose to my feet. By the time I crutched my way out of my bedroom, Noah would be halfway up the stairs, and by the time I made it to the studio, he wouldn't be far behind.

I blinked in surprise, noting the open door to the studio. Had Noah flown up the stairs? Or perhaps my mother had left the door open when she'd been up earlier? I peeked inside. Empty. I conducted a slow one-eighty and waited for footsteps to sound.

Nothing.

I made my way to the exam table and lowered the crutches to the floor. Finally, footfalls reached my ears. My eyes stayed on the empty doorway, waiting for Noah to appear. When he did, he halted as if the force of my gaze held him in place. I swallowed, trying to look simultaneously unassuming and contrite.

Pretty sure a grimace just filled my face instead. "Good morning," I murmured.

"Morning."

"Noah, I—"

"Ms. Ricci, I—"

We started and stopped simultaneously.

Noah made a gesture for me to proceed.

"I am *so* sorry for what I said. I was only teasing, but still, I should have never made a joke out of it."

"Thank you for saying that, but you were right. It *was* unprofessional, and I should never have crossed that line." His ears took on a red tinge as his gaze bounced around the room, looking everywhere but at me.

I was too late. Stilted silence was coming my way.

"I think we should keep things strictly professional. You're paying me to get you back into dancing shape, and I should respect that and act accordingly."

The ache in my chest worsened with each pronouncement.

"I don't want anything to be misconstrued. It'll be best for you *and* for me. I'll call you Ms. Ricci and you can refer to me as Doctor."

I wanted to ask if he did that with his other patients, but didn't dare. I had never seen him this serious. This focused. So much for Celeste thinking he liked me.

"Do you have a problem with anything I've said?" he asked, his green eyes meeting mine for a brief moment.

Yes! I cleared my throat. "No, Doctor." I tried to hide the wince, but it sounded so cold.

How had we gone back so far? I could understand propriety, but virtual strangers?

"And we'll keep all conversation strictly related to your therapy?"

"Yes," I whispered.

His shoulders dropped and a little sigh reached my ears. "That's good. Onto your exercises."

I lay back and followed his requests, trying to keep the heartache from showing on my face. Why should I be so upset? It wasn't like we were friends, but certainly I'd thought we were capable of being friendly toward one another.

Now I was back to feeling all alone in my journey to heal. Noah's calm presence was no longer there to soothe me. Just the robotic doctor here to do what I paid for.

And I wasn't happy. Not one bit.

6

I COULD DELAY NO LONGER. IT HAD BEEN THREE DAYS SINCE MY mother told me to call my father. I stared at the picture of him in my phone's contact profile. The deep-set wrinkles that lined his face but emphasized the happiness in his smile. The muted gray waves that gave him a distinguished air. His features were all so familiar to me, but not in the same way I knew my mother. I could identify my father, but I didn't have a deep understanding of what made him tick. What made him *him.* Being a summer-only daughter, I'd yearned for a deeper connection between us, but always Donnie and Bianca seemed to capture his attention whenever he was around the house and not away on official winery business.

Sadly, I probably knew my stepmother better than my father, as she'd been the one to entertain me all those summers. But I had to straighten up and call him. He would not ask my mother twice—probably because I'd always heeded her.

Picking up my cell, I punched the icon to dial, then placed it against my ear as the phone rang and rang.

"*Piccolina*! About time you call your father."

I smiled at the pet name. Ever since I could remember, my

32

dad had been calling me *little one*. Don and Bianca passed me in height when they turned twelve. Of course, I stopped growing at thirteen. Bianca was now three inches taller than me, and Don currently topped six feet, an inch taller than our father. It was said that I got my height from my paternal grandmother, who'd passed before I was born.

"*Buongiorno, Babbo.*"

"How do you feel? How is your knee?"

Fiery with pain this morning. I'd tried to do my physical therapy on my own, but all it did was make me think of Noah —no, Dr. Wright—and our strange relationship. "It's healing, Babbo."

"Good. Your surgeon was top notch, eh?"

"*Sì*, Babbo. He said the surgery went perfectly and will give me the best chance to dance again."

"Aw, piccolina. I know how much dancing means to you. You dance with your whole heart, but perhaps God is telling you to do something else."

I jerked. "What? Why would you say that?"

"Now, *figlia,* don't be upset with your babbo. I am telling you what I believe is best. Perhaps you should hang up your pointe shoes and marry. You are already twenty-six."

My lips flattened. Wasn't that something a mother should nag about? My father had mastered the art of vexing in a way that brooked no argument, but he was talking about my life. As if dancing were a mere hobby.

"Babbo, you know I can't stop dancing. It means everything to me."

"More than your family? Our God?"

I blinked rapidly as my nose stung with unshed tears. "I can't believe you're saying this to me. I thought you kept calling because you cared."

"I do, piccolina. You are my heart. My first born. I only want what is best for you."

I said nothing. I wanted to believe him, but his actions

said otherwise. He thrived on being a part-time father. Not once had he come to my performances, because they interfered with *his* schedule. He'd only seen replays on news and YouTube.

"I have an idea."

"Yes?"

"Come here for Christmas. You would love it."

"What?" I'd never been to his house for Christmas. Only the summers.

"Sì, you would love it, piccolina. Paulina will cook the most delicious meal, and your brother and sister will be here with their families. You can even bring your friends."

I bit my lip. "I don't know."

"Think about it, sì?"

"Okay. I'll think about it." Christmas was five weeks away. And even though the Macy's parade had come and gone, I felt no Christmas spirit. How could I when my dream was in jeopardy?

"*Bene.* You call me as soon as you decide. There is plenty of room here."

Considering his home was a mansion, yeah, *plenty of room* was an understatement.

"Okay, Babbo. I must go. My therapist will be here soon."

"Therapist?"

I groaned softly. "Physical therapist."

"Aw, okay. I will talk to you later, piccolina."

"*Ciao,* Babbo."

I closed my eyes, picturing Paquita, playing the moves of "Variation #4" over and over until a calm eased my mind. Centered my soul. I couldn't rise into an *arabesque,* one leg pointed back to the sky, the other held *en pointe*. Or perform the pointe steps that were so prevalent in the piece.

But my body remembered the moves. Remembered how time after time I'd practiced, working to execute each move with precise perfection. Knowing I would fall short each and every time but striving, hoping—no, praying—I would come closer to it with each attempt.

I blew out a breath and reached for the crutches. Noah would be here soon for another therapy session, but I needed to speak with Tori and Holiday. I wasn't even sure if they were home. I hobbled over to the intercom and pressed the button to speak.

"You guys home? Hol? Tori?"

"I'm here," Holiday responded. "In my studio. Are you okay?"

"Yes. I just need to ask you a question."

"I'll be right up."

"Where's Tori?"

"Spending the day with Sasha."

Oh good. Sasha was Fox's niece. He had co-guardianship of her with his grandmother. Ever since Tori and Fox had begun fake dating, Tori had taken Sasha under her wing, giving her much needed girl-bonding time.

A few minutes later, Holiday walked into my room and plopped onto the bench at the foot of my bed. "I'm exhausted."

"Why? What's wrong?"

"Trying to finish the last few songs on the Christmas album for next year's release."

"How come you can't release this year?"

"Tavia, the season has already started."

"Right." Thanksgiving had been a low-key affair. I'd been the only one unpaired and the obvious fifth wheel. Needless to say, I hadn't stayed long but spent the rest of the evening in my room streaming shows on my flat screen TV.

"So, what did you want to talk about?"

"My dad invited us to come for Christmas."

"What?" Her eyes widened, and she straightened. "Have you ever been to his house for the holidays?"

"Never."

"Oh, Octavia. What are you going to do?"

I bit my lip. "What do you think I should do? I can't imagine being on a plane for that many hours with my knee the way it is."

"Yes, but we'd most likely leave in a few more weeks. Surely you'll be able to bend it more easily by then. And we can always use a private jet for more leg room."

"True."

"Do you *want* to visit him for Christmas?"

Did I? To see what an Italian Christmas was like? Experience their traditions? "Kind of."

"What does your mom say?"

"I haven't told her." And I didn't know how to. We'd never spent Christmas apart unless the company had an overseas tour.

"Have you prayed about it?" Holiday asked softly.

No. The thought hadn't even crossed my mind. How could I communicate with God when He refused to answer my cries?

"Octavia?" Holiday asked sternly.

"No, I haven't."

She reached out and gripped my hand in hers. "Honey, are you sure you're okay? Do you need to talk?"

I shook my head. What good would talking do? It wouldn't magically heal my knee or earn my spot back as a principal. The one I'd worked dozens of years for, fought the stigma of being an African American ballerina in a world that continued to perpetuate one look for the patrons to see. Earning a principal spot, seeing Misty Copeland lead the charge, it gave me hope that we could bring diversity to the arts.

Show that our bodies held just as much beauty as white men and women.

Now I was out. How long would it take the ballet world to forget me?

"I can't talk right now, Hol. Noah should be arriving soon." I looked away, partially ashamed of my deflection. But Holiday had her own life to worry about. I would be just fine —eventually.

"Ah, the swoon-worthy doctor." Her brown eyes sparkled with amusement.

"Oh please, don't even."

"He's single."

"How do you know?"

"I asked." She blinked owlishly at me. Her big brown eyes made me think of Princess Tiana. Only her hair wasn't up in a bun but fell in loose waves.

"Why? You have Emmett."

"Yes, but one of my best friends just so happens to be single as well."

"Please. I have no time for dating."

Holiday arched an eyebrow, and I rolled my eyes. "Just because I'm not dancing doesn't mean I have time for a relationship."

"That's exactly what it means."

"Ugh. Do not do this to me. I'm not you. I'm not Tori. I don't date."

"That's because dancing took so much of your time. Why not take this golden opportunity and see what's out in the world?"

"He's my doctor."

"If something were to develop, I'm sure you could find another doctor—if that crosses some kind of boundary. It's not like he's your shrink or anything."

"But… "

"But what?" Holiday tilted her head, studying me and trying to see inside my brain.

At least, that's how it felt. "Um, he's white."

She shrugged. "You're half-white."

"Yes, but most people just see my skin color and put me

37

straight in the African American category." I studied the shade of my arms. A nice golden brown that let the world know I was probably mixed, but brown enough to be Black, so they could leave it at that.

"So, what does that matter? There are plenty of interracial couples nowadays."

"Yeah, because that worked out so well for my parents. I mean, obviously my father couldn't handle it. Which is why my stepmom is Italian."

"Tavia!"

"What? I'm not being racist, I'm being realistic. If I dated him, people wouldn't say *Oh she's half-white, so it makes sense.* Someone will call me a sellout."

"But we can't live by others' perceptions, Tavia. I mean, if we did, would you have become a ballerina?"

I squeezed my eyes shut. Pleasing people had been my entire existence. My father loved the ballet—I was a ballerina. My mother wanted me to be a strong Black woman—I never cried in front of others. God wanted me to live a moral life—I made sure not to break the law. Not even a parking citation. You get the picture.

People's expectations were the boundaries of my life. "I just can't, Holiday."

She squeezed my hand. "Don't live for others, Octavia. It's the fastest way to be miserable."

"I'm not." I stared into her eyes. "I'm *not.* I'm good."

Lines crinkled around her eyes. "Are you really?"

"I'll be fine. Promise." I bit my lip and rose unsteadily to my feet.

Holiday stood, her gaze assessing me. "Maybe an Italian Christmas would be good for you."

"If I go, will you?"

"I'll be there if you need me."

I reached out, wrapping my arms around her. "Thank

you." I pulled back. "Let me see if the good doctor is coming."

"And maybe consider giving him a chance."

I snorted and continued walking as if I hadn't heard the asinine suggestion. But the racing of my heart and the tingles going up and down my spine said otherwise.

Noah and I would only ever be *just friends*. There was no other choice.

7

I EXHALED SLOWLY AS I HELD ONTO THE TABLE AND GENTLY BENT my knees. "This is awful!" I groaned.

"Time."

I rose. "Are you sure you're counting correctly? That seemed longer than seven seconds."

"That's because your quad muscles are weak. They often shut off after knee surgery. These exercises are to get them awake and remembering what their function is."

I rolled my eyes. "Fine."

"What happened to *I don't need coddling*?"

"Ten reps of torment happened."

"Pretty good alliteration."

I stifled a laugh. Noah had sensed my tension from the moment he walked in and had been walking some fine line of trying to get me to lighten up while staying within "professional boundaries," but all I could think about was the conversation I'd had with Holiday. How could she think so selfishly? Other people mattered. The Bible told us to esteem others as better, so didn't that mean taking their advice? Not that my mom would ever advise me against interracial relationships, but I wasn't stupid.

I could remember the double-takes my father and I had received every time he introduced me as his daughter. The whispered remarks from my Italian extended family. The looks my own stepmother threw my way. Why would I want any child of mine to have to experience and live through that kind of hurt? Besides, who said Noah was even interested in me? I didn't know much about him, other than his teenage rebellious streak. Which reminded me…

"You never finished telling me how your parents got you into the concierge doctor business."

His soulful green eyes studied me. "You're right. I didn't." He cleared his throat. "Remember, it's better that we keep things professional between us, Ms. Ricci."

Ouch, he was going for the jugular.

"Next exercise."

I resisted the urge to roll my eyes at his brusqueness and started another round of repetitions. "You know, I would consider it a *professional* courtesy if you'd distract me from the pain you're inflicting on me. Not to mention, we're literally discussing your profession. Nothing about my personal life or yours."

He grunted softly and ran a hand through his hair. "When you put it that way… My parents, uh, knew someone. Someone famous who was injured. Told them how I was a physical therapist. I'd had my doctorate for a year, so I was feeling a bit special."

I smiled.

"He asked my boss for me specifically and asked if I would come to his home so he didn't have to come into the clinic."

"And your boss agreed?"

"After he heard the figure the guy offered to pay? Whole-heartedly."

I giggled. "But you work for yourself now."

"I do. The client referred me to his friends, and soon word

spread. I couldn't keep my client list at the clinic with my new concierge list. Had to do some praying before coming to the decision that I was better at one-on-one therapy."

"You're a believer?"

"Caught that, did you?"

I huffed out a breath as I switched to the next exercise. "I did."

"Worried my broken arm rebellion meant I was uncouth?"

I stopped mid exercise, clutching my stomach with laughter. Just hearing him say the word threw my imagination into fits. "You are the farthest from uncouth that I can imagine."

"I was dangerous back then."

"Yeah, to yourself. Your poor arm."

"Ouch, you wound me." He grabbed his chest as if I'd hit him. He showed me the next exercise. "I gave my mom a lot of gray hairs, you know."

"Sure you did." I grinned.

We were back. No awkwardness, just an ease that was perfectly friendly and perfectly respectful.

If I could just tell my pulse to keep at an even beat and not go full speed ahead, then maybe my hormones would believe I didn't want more than this moment right now.

"Oh, she'd happily tell you all the drama I put her through."

"What about your dad? What stories would he tell me?"

A downcast turn filled his eyes. "He passed away shortly after I started my business."

"I'm sorry, Noah."

And just like that, his emotions shuttered and that fake professional façade came back.

He cleared his throat. "I think we're about done here, Ms. Ricci."

"Noah—"

"*Dr.* Wright." His tone wasn't harsh, but the resolve in his words was like a papercut to my heart.

"Right. Sorry." I stared down at the ground, willing myself to remain calm.

With bewildering efficiency, he ended our appointment and left me to my own devices. It appeared Dr. Wright was here to stay and Noah was no more.

A WEEK HAD PASSED, AND STILL MY RELATIONSHIP WITH NOAH didn't budge from Dr. and Ms. It maddened everything inside me and put me on edge. I whipped the fridge door open, shuffling food left and right, trying to find something edible.

"What is wrong with you?" Holiday called from over my shoulder.

I turned and gave her a look. You know the kind you give someone when they're between you and food? Only she was on the other side of the island—safe. "I'm hungry."

"Girl, that amount of 'tude goes beyond hungry."

"Are you going to help me find something to eat or just waste my time with nonsense?"

Holiday's eyes widened.

I closed my eyes. "I'm sorry, Hol." I rubbed the spot between my brow.

"Probably all that bird food. Starvation finally sank in."

My lips quirked. "It's healthy. You have to treat your body right if you want it to treat you right."

Holiday smirked. "I'm doing just fine thanks."

"Now. Wait until you hit your forties."

"Don't say such a dirty word."

I giggled and sighed. "I really am sorry."

"I know. But seriously, eat a brownie and you'll feel much better."

I grabbed one out of the cake dish and bit into it. When I opened my eyes, Holiday was staring at me in horror.

"What?" I asked after swallowing.

"You didn't heat it up or put ice cream on it."

"It's a brownie."

"Oh, my, word. Such a travesty. No wonder you're going around here snapping at people."

"I just said I was sorry," I snapped. Regret coursed through me, so I took another bite of the brownie.

"I'm not talking about me. Tori said she was over yesterday grabbing something she'd forgotten, and you almost bit her head off." She held up a hand. "Her words, not mine."

I remembered the exchange.

Tori had walked into my bathroom to get her old curling iron. Even though she told me why she was in my room, I still lost all sense and expressed my displeasure. She pretended to knock me upside my head with the curling iron, muttering about "needs some sense knocked into her before I lose all cool and remind her I'm not one to be messed with."

And she'd continued muttering all the way out of the room.

"I sent her an apology via text."

"You doing a lot of apologizing, huh?"

If people would just leave me alone...but I couldn't say that to Holiday. Didn't even really mean it. I took another bite of the brownie then met her gaze. "Sorry?"

Holiday shook her head. "Well, whatever *is* wrong, you know where to find me when you're ready to talk."

"Thanks."

"Anytime, Tavia." She waved and waltzed out of the room.

Probably putting ample distance between herself and my temper. I sighed. I didn't know how to shake this funk. It wasn't like I could talk it out with Noah, since he wanted to keep everything strictly business.

I scoffed and reached for another brownie. This time, I grabbed a bowl, stuffed it in the microwave for a few seconds, then searched the fridge for the French vanilla ice cream. After dishing up a couple of scoops, I took bite. I moaned with pleasure.

Holiday was right.

Warm brownies were made for ice cream.

❧ 8 ❧

"YOU HAVE TO GET OUT OF THIS HOUSE."

I groaned as Tori shook my shoulders. "There are too many stairs," I whined.

"Fox is willing to carry you down."

My face burned. "He's your husband. It feels weird."

"Then I can get Emmett."

I huffed. "He's engaged to Holiday."

"Well, excuse me. Your *good doctor* isn't available."

"He's not mine."

"Don't you wish."

I could practically hear the smirk in my friend's voice. "Tori, I thought married life would keep you away."

"Ouch."

I winced and slowly maneuvered into an upright position. "I'm sorry." I laid a hand on her arm, contrite that I'd hurt one of my best friends.

"I know the whole knee situation has been difficult—"

"But I shouldn't let that turn me into a shrew."

Tori gasped, her eyes appearing blue in her caramel-colored face. "I was *not* going to say that." She paused. "Even if I thought it."

I giggled. "Love you."

"I love you too, Tavia." She hugged me. "Please, shower and get out of this house. I promise we'll have fun."

"You're right. I'll get up."

"Thank you, God."

I shook my head in bemusement. Never had I thought to hear my girlfriends thank God or even suggest I pray. They'd gone about their lives without Him as long as I'd known them, but over this past year, both had accepted Him into their lives.

Sometimes a part of me believed He'd left me to minister to them. And shouldn't that make me happy? Instead, I had to push down the jealousy that they were connecting to Him and I was all alone.

Enough, Octavia. Buck up. Live again.

I went through my morning routine. Not the same as the old one that would have had me on the rooftop doing yoga and then in the studio practicing my performance moves before leaving to attend the company's sessions. Now my morning was spent going through Noah's stretches, all the while grimacing at the fire and permanent ache in my leg.

Afterward, I made my way into the walk-in shower, thankful my bathroom suite had a separate tub so I didn't have to step over the sides to get clean. Taking Tori's suggestion to heart, I opted for the bare essentials of makeup—a sweep of mascara and a pink gloss over my lips. I let my hair hang down past my shoulders.

Angling my head left then right, a thought popped in my head. Maybe I should get a haircut. Short enough to ease the burden of dead weight and long enough to still be able to pull back off my face. My hair held a natural curl, but I always straightened it to ease my strands into a bun. I bit my lip, assessing the situation. *We'll see.*

I searched through the racks of clothes in my closet for something that would allow me to wear the knee brace but also appear somewhat sophisticated, since I'd be stepping out of the house with Tori and possibly Holiday—I forgot to ask.

A wrap dress would do. I pulled on the black sheath with the pale-pink floral pattern. Leggings came next. Thankfully, the tugging motion didn't hurt my knee as much as I'd thought it would. I put on the knee brace next for support, then grabbed my jacket and crutched my way back into the bedroom from my closet. My crossbody purse would work best. I wouldn't have to worry about holding it up on my shoulder as I crutched through Manhattan—or wherever we were going.

It wasn't Sunday, so no brunch. Maybe a spa day?

A rap of knuckles interrupted my thoughts. "Come in," I yelled.

"Hey, Tavia, your chariot awaits."

I peeked around the corner and grinned at Emmett. "Hey, you're the lucky one?"

"Tori said we needed to spread the wealth."

Sweet of her not to divulge the real reason for my discomfort. I hated that I had to rely on my friends' significant others to take me down the stairs.

What would it be like if Noah swept me into his arms and carried me to the first floor? Would I swoon like a historical heroine or declare my independence as a contemporary one?

Not that Noah was my hero in any case.

Just a doctor. *Only* my doctor.

Maybe I should ask my mom why she and my father had split apart. Reconfirm my belief that interracial relationships were filled with more heartache than not. Look at Prince Harry and his duchess. She was half Black like me and had been slaughtered in the newsstands because of that, her divorced past, and being from America.

Yeah, nationalities at war once again.

I shook off my thoughts as Emmett asked if I was ready. "Yes."

He picked me up, and I held on to my crutches. "Do you know where we're going, Emmett?"

"Serendipity's and then a game." He huffed as he descended the stairs.

I loved Serendipity's frozen hot chocolate. It was magic in a cup and a perfect way to bring me some Christmas cheer. "Hockey game?"

"You know it." He let out a breath as we headed for the first floor.

"Oh no! I forgot my gloves and scarf."

Emmett lowered me to the ground. "Do you want me to grab them for you?"

"No, that's okay."

"What's wrong?" Holiday walked into the hallway from the living room, looking stunning as usual. She kissed Emmett on the cheek.

"Octavia was saying she should have grabbed her gloves and scarf. I was about to run up and get them."

Holiday scanned me up and down, taking in my outfit. "I can run up and grab those for you. It's not a problem."

"Thanks." I gave her a sheepish grin as I leaned onto my crutches.

"Be right back." She skirted up the curved staircase, and Emmett picked me up and finished descending to the ground floor.

By the time Holiday came back down, Fox and Tori had joined us in the hallway. They had some fleece blankets with them. I couldn't help but eye the pairs and wish I were part of one. Maybe I should join a dating app or get an online profile. I still wasn't sold on the idea of dating, but this fifth-wheel business had to go.

I didn't want to be bitter or jealous around my best friends. If only the Lord would bring me someone so I didn't have to feel the isolation so starkly.

Noah entered my mind. How calm he was. How carefree I

felt in those moments when his guard was down and the teasing flowed between us. If only he weren't white.

Ugh, why did race have to matter so much? Why couldn't I just like a guy to like him?

I bit my lip and followed my friends out of the house. Fox and Emmett each took me by the arm and carried me down the front steps while Holiday held onto my crutches. Once in the car, I settled back into my seat, thankful I could sit with my leg extended.

"People are going to take lots of pictures of me, aren't they?"

"Probably." Holiday gave me a pitying look.

"Don't. I'll be fine."

"Are you sure?" Tori asked. "We could go back. I just thought escaping the house might help."

I smiled at her. "It will. I appreciate it. Promise."

She sighed and leaned back. "I'm sorry, Octavia. More than I can ever say."

"It's not your fault." I peered into Tori's eyes.

She'd been riddled with guilt ever since I'd been injured. And yes, part of me struggled in the forgiveness arena, but she didn't have to know that. Intellectually, I knew my injury wasn't her fault. She hadn't been the one to attack me. But it had been *her* stalker.

Lord, please take that thought away. Please keep our relationship intact through this whole ordeal.

I couldn't lose one of my best friends. I had so few acquaintances outside of ballet that the ones who managed to become more were coveted. I needed the sisterhood Holiday and Tori had offered since the moment we'd all agreed to be BFFs.

"You can walk between us. Then maybe the gawkers won't get a great shot," Holiday suggested.

"Sounds perfect." Tori nodded.

"Thanks, guys."

"Anytime," they parroted.

The car pulled to a stop, and Holiday got out first, then me, with Tori quickly taking the space next to me. Murmurs went through the crowd lined along the curb waiting for entry.

"We already booked a table online, so we shouldn't have to wait," Holiday said as we strode forward.

"Wonderful."

People started calling out Holiday's and Tori's names. They both ignored the onlookers and kept walking until we entered the specialty restaurant.

The mouthwatering scent of chocolate greeted me, and I dragged in a deep breath. "The humiliation of being carried down the stairs was so worth it."

Holiday chuckled. "I don't know what you have to be embarrassed about. You weigh as much as a child."

"Truth," Tori grumbled.

"How about the part where I can't walk down the stairs on my own steam? Something I've been able to do since I was a toddler."

"There is that," Tori agreed.

Fox stepped forward and gave our names, and soon the hostess led us to a table. The smell of mint and chocolate floated in the air.

I stopped abruptly. Noah sat at a corner booth, eating wings and grinning at a woman seated across from him.

"Are you okay?" Holiday asked.

I gulped. "Just fine." I started moving again but couldn't prevent my gaze from drifting to Noah once more.

His gaze roamed the restaurant and locked onto mine. I came to a halt, picturing the stunning green color of his eyes in my mind. How much they made my pulse pound with just one look.

Noah waved hesitantly.

I waved back, breath suspended as I wondered what would happen next.

"Is that Noah?" Holiday asked.

I nodded, looking quickly at Holiday.

"Why don't you go over and say hello?"

"I can't go over there."

"Sure you can." Holiday gave me a light shove. "Don't forget to smile," she whispered.

As I crutched my way over to him, I ran greeting after greeting in my head. *Hi, Noah.* Too plain.

What's up, Doc? Horribly cheesy. *How are you?* Not bad.

I stopped at his table.

"Hi," he murmured.

"Hello." *So not what you practiced.*

"You look good." His face reddened. "I mean, it's good to see you out of the house. Getting fresh air." He cleared his throat and stood. "Uh, this is my mother." He gestured across from him, and I turned to see his mom.

Her dark brown hair fell in soft waves, stopping at her shoulders. Her pale skin had artfully applied makeup to give her a soft blush across her high cheekbones, and her bright pink lipstick matched her sweater. Lines fanned out around her eyes as she smiled.

"Hi, I'm Octavia."

"Right, that's what I was about to say." Noah placed a hand in the middle of his chest, clearing his throat once more. "Mom, this is a client of mine, Octavia Ricci. Octavia, my mom."

"Nice to meet you, Mrs. Wright."

"Oh, no, you can call me Rina."

"Thank you." I studied Noah, waiting for him to fill the awkward silence, but he remained mute. "Well, I'm going to go join my friends. I hope you have a good day."

"You too. You're okay, right?" He leaned in, his voice low and soothing.

I wanted to lean right back toward him but held in my breath as I nodded.

"Good." He gave another little cough. "It really was... uh...good to see you."

"Likewise. Bye, Noah."

I hurried away before I could prolong the torture and stare more into his dreamy puppy-dog eyes.

❦ 9 ❧

Madison Square Garden had been turned into a hockey arena. Thousands of fans stomped their feet to Queen's "We Will Rock You" as the New York Rangers and New York Islanders took to the ice. I followed my friends through the arena. Adrenaline pumped inside me as the guitar riff pumped through the speakers.

Tori hit the elevator button then snuggled into Fox's side. Holiday and Emmett's hands were entwined as they made eyes at one another.

How nauseating.

I appreciated my friends wanting to get me out of the house, but the least they could do was tone down the PDA. Seeing them all lovey-dovey snuggly was getting to be a bit much.

"Octavia?"

I froze, then slowly turned to look over my shoulder. *Noah?* What were the odds of seeing him among the millions that roamed the city's streets, let alone twice in just a couple of hours?

"Noah?"

He smiled, sliding his hands into his pockets. He broke

away from the couple he'd been standing next to. "Can't believe we keep running into each other."

"What are the odds?"

He shrugged, looking down at his feet. "Who knows?"

This awkwardness was killing me. I swallowed. "Where's your mom?"

"Hockey's not her thing. But my cousin and his wife love the Rangers." He gestured behind him to the couple taking an obvious interest in our conversation.

My cheeks heated at their scrutiny, and I reverted my gaze back to the shuffling doctor. "Where are you guys sitting?"

"Tavia, coming?"

I looked behind me to see Tori holding the elevator. I waved her away and she nodded, removing her hand to let the doors close. I'd head up to the suite we rented for the winter season later.

"Uh…" Noah faltered as our gazes locked. "I forget."

"Maybe it says on your ticket?"

"Huh." A smirk played over his lips as he looked down, pulling his ticket out of his wallet. He relayed the section his seats were in.

Not as good as our view. I bit my lip, glancing at his cousins then back to him. "Would you like to join me and my friends? We have enough space in our suite."

His eyes bugged out. "Are you serious?"

"Of course. Have you ever watched a game from box seating?"

"Not at all."

"Then join me. I mean, *us*. It'll be fun." I grinned as if my smile would prove my words true.

"I—well, if you're sure," he stated cautiously.

"Very."

"Then, thank you." He motioned for his cousins to join our conversation.

The woman must have been reading our lips or something, because she dashed forward, sticking her hand out in greeting. "Hi, I'm Lisa."

"Octavia."

"So nice to meet you." A blush flamed over her cheeks. "You're, like, my favorite ballerina."

"Really?" Delight filled me. It was rare for me to meet fans. I was used to always seeing Holiday's and Tori's, not my own.

"Dead serious. I've seen every performance you've ever been in. If not in person, then on YouTube." She grinned sheepishly.

"I'm honored. I was just telling Noah that you two—and him of course—should join me and my friends. We have a suite."

"We'd love to, right, honey?" Lisa fluttered her eyelashes as she peered up at her husband.

"Sure. Yes."

"Uh…" Noah pointed. "James, Lisa, this is Octavia. Octavia, my cousins."

"Nice to meet you," we all chorused.

I smiled and moved to hit the up button on the elevator, but Noah beat me to it as he saw me crutch in that direction.

"Thanks again," he murmured.

"Sure. The more the merrier, right?" And I wouldn't have to be a fifth wheel.

"Right."

The door chimed and we filed in, silence descending as the doors slid closed.

"Thanks again for inviting us," Lisa said.

"It's my pleasure."

Lisa's gaze widened. "Um, will there be other ballerinas there?"

"Actually, my roommates. I share a house with Holiday Brown and Astoria Fox."

"Oh, my—" Lisa gasped for air as her hands mimed clutching her heart.

"Are you a fan?" I asked, trying to hold back my laughter.

Lisa nodded her head excitedly.

"Great. Then you'll have fun with us."

"Uh, yeah!"

Noah chuckled, rubbing the back of his neck. "I hope she doesn't embarrass us," he whispered, "but if she does, I apologize in advance."

"No problem," I murmured back, suppressing a shiver as his breath caressed my cheek.

The door opened and we headed to the suite. I quickly introduced everyone, Lisa watching in fangirl delight and Noah and James in barely contained amusement. Soon, we all had snacks prepared by our awesome chef and were settled in to watch the game. Fox had placed an ottoman for me to elevate my leg, which meant I couldn't peer out the glass, but I could watch from the flat screen TV hanging on the wall.

"Mind if I join you?" Noah gestured to the empty seat beside me.

"Wouldn't you rather watch from the glass partition?"

He tipped up his left shoulder. "I'm good."

"Then by all means."

He flashed a smile as he sat down with his plate of nachos. "The suite life is pretty amazing."

"It is. I often take it for granted."

"If this is how you grew up, I could see how that's possible."

"How did you grow up?" I bit my lip, suddenly feeling awkward.

He swallowed his bite before speaking. "In an apartment in Brooklyn with my mom and dad. But my grandparents, aunts and uncles, and cousins all lived in our building as well. A closed door was merely a suggestion."

I chuckled at the look of chagrin on his face. "No privacy?"

"None."

"It's like that when I go back to Italy. My cousins are often in and out, and no space is sacred."

"Exactly. The curse of big families." Noah stopped and looked at his cousins. "But we wouldn't have it any other way, would we?"

I sidestepped the question with one of my own. "Did you ever feel lonely despite their constant presence?" Why had I asked that? I looked down at my food, moving my fruit around with my fork.

"More than I'd care to admit."

At Noah's solemn proclamation, my head jerked up. "Really?"

"How could I not? Even though they were my family, I was very much aware I was an only child. And I'm still different than the majority of my cousins. I'm the only doctor in the family."

"Are you? I'm the only ballerina."

"But that's something extraordinary."

"So is being a doctor."

His face flushed, ears bright red with embarrassment. "I feel the need to hide my face from you the majority of the time."

"Why?"

"I get embarrassed way too easily around you."

"I'm not keeping a catalog of the number of times you blush."

"Men don't blush."

I held in my chuckle at the seriousness coating his words. And ignored the shiver of awareness at his declaration. "Noah?"

"Hmm?"

"What do you call it when someone's cheeks redden?"

"Blushing…*if* you're a girl."

I laughed outright. "I thought I almost had you there."

"Gotta be quicker on your feet, Octavia." He winced and blushed. "Uh, I meant that figuratively not literally. I'm going to shut up." He stuffed a tortilla chip covered with toppings into his mouth.

It shouldn't have been appealing. Gorging oneself on food should be as far away from attractive as possible. But the embarrassment and need to take his foot out of his mouth sent my hormones into multiple *grand jetés*.

I shoved a piece of strawberry into my mouth. I needed to remind myself why Noah and I would never work.

1. He was my doctor. I was his patient.
2. He was white. I was not.
3. We grew up differently.

Ugh, my list sucked. Those reasons seemed so superficial. Maybe I needed to ask him deep questions to find some difference that couldn't be overcome.

Race is a fatal flaw. Hello, remember your parents. Remember the comments your relatives said about not being a real Italian.

"Octavia?"

"Yes?" I met Noah's concerned gaze.

"I asked if you were okay?"

"Oh yes. Just lost in thought." I offered what I hoped was a reassuring smile.

"If it's about my comment before, I—"

"Do you ever wonder if some differences are too hard to overcome?"

He cocked his head, studying me as if searching for any hidden meaning to my question. "I think anything can be overcome."

"How?"

"With love. After all, God is love, and Jesus told us anything is possible with God."

God and love. Two things I wasn't sure about at the moment. "Do you really believe that?"

Noah leaned forward, placing his plate on the table beside him and resting his arms on his knees. "In my head, yes. But some days, it's harder to believe. Those are the days I pray the hardest and the most."

"But what if you can't hear Him?" My voice came out as soft as a whisper.

"Then be still and listen to His voice."

I stared at Noah, searching for the words to offer my gratitude. That he would delve deeper than I'd dared hope and offer a connection I hadn't felt in…well, forever. But my heart had swelled in size and my tongue was rendered useless.

Instead, I reached out to squeeze his hand and he sandwiched his palms over mine. Heat spread from the contact, warming my heart and soothing my worries. For one beautiful moment, all was right, and I didn't want to think any further than that.

10

NOAH STROLLED INTO THE ROOM AND MY BREATH CAUGHT. Would he treat me like he had when we watched hockey together? Letting his guard down and letting me in? Or were we back to our Dr. and Ms. relationship?

"Morning. How are you feeling?"

"Fine."

"A sincere fine or one of your *I don't want to burden another with my true feelings* fines?"

I giggled. "A real fine. I took some pain killers and a nice hot shower. Worked all the tension out." Except for the strain of knowing which Noah was talking.

"Good. So you're ready for some exercises?"

"Sure."

Without delay, he launched into a visual of a new exercise that would get my knee bending in a natural way instead of forced. "Now you do it."

I blinked. That was it? No "The game was great. My cousins had a good time"? We were just going to pretend like the weekend had never happened? Like he hadn't looked into my soul and offered hope for internal healing?

I repeated his instructions, trying to keep from grimacing at the uncomfortable pinch in my leg.

"Does it hurt?"

"Just uncomfortable."

"Remember to breathe."

"Right. Ballerinas never forget."

His lips twitched as if fighting a full-fledged smile.

I wanted to clap my hands. The same Noah I saw at the hockey game was in there, and I was convinced he was dying to get out. To move from this need to be super professional and maybe even settle into friends.

Because friends was as far as I was willing to take it.

I peeked at him. "So…I've met Lisa and James. How many other cousins do you have?"

He blinked, his Adam's apple bopping up then down. "Ms. Ricci, I really think we should keep things professional in the therapy room."

"And knowing how many cousins you have is unprofessional? I mean, for goodness' sake, we watched a hockey game together yesterday. We were using first names. And now you're back to Ms. Ricci this and Ms. Ricci that?"

I wanted to slap a hand over my mouth, hating the snappish tone in my voice. But enough really was enough.

Noah blew out a breath. "I'm sorry."

"So am I. I shouldn't have talked to you like that."

"I honestly didn't know how to handle the whole hockey game then coming back to work."

"I mean, we're friends now, right?"

"Are we?"

"I'd like to be." Being friendly with others was what was expected, right?

A small smile crested his face, and my heart did a *pirouette*. What was it about this man that had me tiptoeing out of my comfort zone? I truly didn't want a romantic relationship, and I never wanted to endure the hardships my parents had.

But I couldn't deny there was something about Dr. Noah Wright that piqued my interested just a bit.

"Friends?" He stuck out his hand.

I couldn't stop the smile from spreading across my face. "Friends."

"Good. Now get back to work. You still have two more reps."

"Ugh. Just as long as you remember you owe me an answer."

"No whining or I'll add more."

I froze. "You wouldn't."

"I would."

"Fine." I rolled my eyes and gripped the end of the table, slowly lowering my knees into a miniature squat. "Cousins?"

"Quite a few."

That made sense. He did mention a big family. "Were you born in New York?"

"Brooklyn. Time."

I straightened my knees, pushing out a breath at the same time.

"Ready to go again?"

Did I have a choice? I nodded.

"Go." There was a brief pause. "Were you born in New York?"

"Actually, *Italia*."

Both Noah's eyebrows rose in an adorable fashion. "Time." He crossed his arms across his lean frame. "Do you have dual citizenship?"

"Yes. It was easy to get since my mom is a US citizen."

"I imagine so. Do you go back to Italy a lot?"

"It depends." I sighed and sat on the exam table. "Last time was for my half-sister's wedding. Growing up, I went every summer."

"Do you have just the half-sister?"

"Half-brother as well. They're twins."

"When will you go back again?"

"Actually…" I exhaled. "My father wants me to come for Christmas."

"And that bothers you?"

"How could you tell?"

"You bite your lip when you get anxious." He pointed to the corner of my mouth where I'd been nibbling.

My cheeks heated under his scrutiny. "I never knew anyone noticed."

He shrugged as if embarrassed for knowing something about me. But wasn't that what friends did—pick up those little nuances that made us *us?* "He invited my friends too. If I end up going, it would be nice if they came too." Erase the awkwardness I was sure would be there with my other family.

"Have they met your dad?"

"My dad, yes. The others, no."

"How many others?"

"So many others." I giggled.

"Big families are the best in my opinion. That's why it's so odd that I'm an only child."

"Was that by choice?"

He shook his head. "No, my mom had some medical issues."

"I'm sorry."

"I appreciate that. She calls me her miracle baby."

"And spoils you rotten?"

His cheeks reddened. "Maybe. But I try not to act spoiled."

"Sure you do." I laughed as he rubbed the back of his neck. "Are we done for the day, Doc?"

"Noah," he grunted. "You can call me Noah."

I tried not to show my pleasure. Didn't need to scare him off and have him take it back, so I tried for a joke. "Doc Noah."

"Smart aleck."

I giggled. "Who says that?"

"I try to keep my language clean."

"Do you say fiddlesticks, cheese and crackers, and other nonsense?"

Noah's face had flushed to a nice shade of red.

"Oh my goodness, you do!" I let out a full laugh, clutching my sides. "This is too great."

A part of me felt bad for teasing him so mercilessly, but another part loved how the green of his eyes deepened when he was embarrassed. How his hair stuck up in various places from running his fingers through it.

"Do friends laugh at each other?" he asked in a sulking tone.

"We do."

"Do we now?"

I sat up straight, eyeing him warily. "Maybe I should say *I* laugh."

"Oh no. An equal opportunity friendship in the teasing department is a must."

"I've created a monster," I whispered.

"Roar!"

My lips twitched. "Goodbye, Noah. Go harass your other patients."

"Nope." He glanced at his watch. "We can fit in a few more exercises."

I nodded, and he demonstrated another one. And another. And finally gave me the last exercise of the day.

"Did you bring ice?"

"I did." He pulled the ice pack out of the mini freezer and placed it on my knee, then tilted the exam table so I was slightly hanging upside down. "Leave it on for about fifteen minutes."

"Sounds good." I was no stranger to the ice game. I'd been

using it on my feet and various ballet-related injuries for years now.

"Have you made a decision regarding your dad's offer?"

"Not really." And the indecision was one of the things ruining my sleep.

"And Ms. Bell and Ms. Brown will go with you?"

"I don't know. And Tori is Fox now."

"How did you three even become friends?"

I shrugged. "We went to boarding school together. Celebrity circles are a lot smaller than you think."

"Why did you decide to move in together? I mean, surely you all can afford your own places."

"Sure, but we were eighteen and didn't want to live at home any longer. Or alone. I think our parents were a little relieved that we wanted to share a house together."

"Good point. Not sure I'd want my daughter living alone in the city."

"Do you have kids?" I peaked at him from beneath my lashes.

"Nope. Never been married."

"Never ever?"

"Not even engaged."

"How old are you?"

"Wow, we moved quickly into this friends business, didn't we?"

I covered my laugh. "We're on hyper speed."

"Nerd."

I rolled my eyes. "Age, Noah. Age."

"Thirty."

"And a doctor? So young."

"Well, physical therapy is different than being a medical doctor or surgeon."

"True."

"How old are you?"

"Twenty-six."

"Kind of young."

"Seriously?"

He rubbed his head. "I mean, were we even in high school at the same time?"

"When did you graduate?"

He said the year and I laughed. "I was only three years behind you, so there."

"How?"

"I skipped a grade."

"So you *are* a nerd."

I tipped a shoulder. "I like math."

"Huh."

"What? What does that noise mean?"

"Just surprised me that's all. You're a ballerina, so I figured you would be into other artsy things like literature."

My lips curled up. "Books kind of bore me."

"Ouch." He clutched his heart. "Our whole friendship needs to be reevaluated."

"But *I'm* the nerd?"

"Touché."

"How can you stand it? Just reading words. I'd rather watch a movie."

"But everyone knows books are better than movies."

"Says who? Book nerds, that's who."

He laughed, and the joy echoing in the studio warmed my heart. He had a wonderful laugh. I closed my eyes, trying to push the delightful sound away before I fell under his spell any further.

"Are you done with the ice? You in pain?"

"I'm fine." I kept my eyes closed.

"But you've got lines crossing your forehead like you're *not* fine."

I exhaled. "I promise, the ice is nothing. It's not even time for me to take meds yet."

"You sure?"

"I'm okay, Doc."

"There you go again. You can tell me the truth."

"Promise. I'm fine." I lifted up on my elbows. "You know, I think I'm done for the day."

He eyed me warily. "Okay then. I'll leave and see you Friday."

I nodded, biting the inside of my lip, hoping the nervous tick wouldn't show. "See you then."

Hopefully by then I'd have put him back into the friends-only box and forgotten how much my pulse raced in his presence.

11

THE CRISP WINTER AIR CARESSED MY FACE AS I INHALED, FILLING my lungs to full capacity before exhaling as slowly as possible. I repeated the breathing techniques until the quietness of the morning took over my senses and the thoughts in my head dulled to a whisper. I couldn't do my regular yoga routine, but I could concentrate on breathing. I could focus on being still.

The darkness of the morning shrouded me while, in my mind, I pictured the heavenly throne room. The magnificent colors surrounding our Creator, shining from Him, brightening everything the light hit. Warmth soaked my heart as I pictured myself, kneeled before Him without pain. My chest to my knees as I bowed before the King.

Help me be still. I miss You. Miss Your voice. Miss Your presence. Where did You go?

The thought echoed in my mind as I continued to picture the beauty of heaven. When was the last time I'd sat like this —connecting with my Heavenly Father the only thought on my mind?

I'm sorry. For being so busy with ballet that I forgot You were

*my first love. I forgot to seek You first above all. I forgot how much
You want a relationship with me.*

I bit my lip in contemplation. The Creator of the universe
wanted a relationship with me. How had I taken that for
granted? When had I pushed Him to the back corners of my
mind when all along, I should have been running to Him? It
had taken a potentially career-ending injury to help me re-
prioritize.

*I'm sorry for ignoring You. For putting ballet before You. Please
forgive me. Please help me to know what truly matters.*

My head dipped low and focused on the light of God to
keep my mind clear. It had been a while since I'd practiced
silence—something I always struggled with because my brain
was like a laptop with tons of tabs open and vying for attention. To purposely close them all out and just leave my God
tab open made me uncomfortable. Not because of who He
was, but because of me.

The need to constantly be doing something, anything, was
how I lived my life. Now I was stuck resting and healing. Life
had slowed down tremendously, and I didn't know how to
deal with that.

My cell vibrated, breaking my concentration. My father's
face flashed on the screen. I hadn't come to a decision about
Christmas, but I couldn't avoid his calls any longer. I swiped
the answer icon, placing the phone against my ear. "Buongiorno, Babbo."

"Buongiorno, piccolina. How are you?"

I looked out at neighboring rooftops. "I'm okay. You?"

"Better now that I hear your sweet voice."

Wow, he was pulling out all the charm.

"Have you thought about Christmas?"

"I have."

"What did you decide, piccolina?"

*Curse of the big families. But we wouldn't have it any other
way, would we?*

Noah's words floated in my head like a cautionary tale reminding me to think before I spoke. "I will be there, Babbo."

"Mamma mia! You have made your babbo very happy, piccolina."

I smiled at the enthusiasm in his voice. "When should I come?"

"How 'bout you spend Christmas and New Year's with us, eh?"

More than a week in Italia? It wasn't as long as my summer vacations had been. I smiled. This would be my first time seeing the sights in winter. "Okay. I'll find the best flight and see when the girls can get away too."

"No flights. You tell me the dates, and I will send the jet for you, *tutto bene*?"

"Okay. *Grazie,* Babbo."

"*Prego,* piccolina. Call me with dates, sì?"

"Sì. I will."

"*Addio.*"

"Ciao, Babbo."

Christmas in Tuscany. The girls would be excited, and hopefully the guys too. I frowned, realizing that meant I would once more be the fifth wheel.

Uffa. It couldn't be helped.

I texted my mom.

O: Can you come help me?

M: Be right up

O: Thank you

Earlier, my mom had helped me navigate the stairs from the fifth floor to the rooftop so that I could have my quiet time. Tomorrow, I might have to practice peace in my room instead of poking the bear that was my mother during her sleeping hours. She hated to wake early.

"Tavi, where are you?"

I twisted, waving my mom toward my spot.

"Oh, why is it so dark up here?"

"I didn't turn on the light. Wanted to just enjoy the atmosphere."

"Atmosphere?" My mom arched an eyebrow, mouth curling as if the word left a bad aftertaste on her tongue.

I giggled. "It gives me peace."

"Hmm. Get on up, now." She lifted me by the forearms, and I stood on my feet, placing my weight on the right.

She hurriedly handed me the crutches, and I sank onto the rubber supporters, easing the fire in my left leg. "Thank you."

"Sure. Is this going to be a daily occurrence? You know I need my beauty sleep."

"Whatever. But no. I won't wake you up daily."

"Thank the good Lord for small favors."

"Mom?"

"Yes, dear?"

"I told Dad I would visit him for the holidays."

She halted, her dark-brown eyes assessing my features. "You're okay with that?"

"I'm more worried you won't be."

"I'll be fine." She waved a hand in the air. "'Bout time you two explored the other months of the year together."

"Really? You're not upset?" I hadn't expected this reaction.

"Tavia, you're not just my child. He's your father, and I imagine he's hated not having you with him all these years."

"Then why is this the first time he's asked for me to visit during Christmas?" It had been one of the reasons I'd almost said no. Years of hurt had built upon themselves, making me slightly bitter and resentful when it came to Donovan Ricci.

My mother let out a puff of air. "That's not exactly true."

"What do you mean?" What was she talking about?

"He used to ask when you were younger."

"What?" My heart double-timed as if I were performing *sissonne*. "Why is this the first time I'm hearing this?"

"I was in a bad place for a while, Tavi. Don't you remember how much I used to complain about him?"

I dipped my head, not wanting to make her feel any worse, but I couldn't lie either.

"Part of my frustration was because he wanted more visitation rights. Finally, I won out because of your dedication to ballet."

The one thing I'd done to please my father had kept me from him? My mouth dropped. "Are you serious?"

"I am. I'm so sorry, sweetie. I never wanted to hurt you."

"Just help me get to my room." I'd deal with my feelings later.

"Tavia, let's talk about this."

"Not now." I shook my head, concentrating on going down the steps without injuring myself further. "I need to process this alone."

"Can you forgive me?" Her voice was small, sorrow tingeing her words and cloaking the staircase with misery.

"Eventually," I replied.

And then I walked the rest of the way into my bedroom, closing the door behind me and shutting the world out.

12

THE GIRLS STARED AT ME IN SHOCK AS I RELAYED WHAT MY mother had told me.

"So she never let him have you for any other holiday?" Holiday's brow furrowed.

"Never. Claimed she was in a bad place."

"That's an understatement," Tori shot out. "How are you dealing with this?"

I groaned, leaning against my velvet headboard. "I'm not sure what to think. On the one hand, I'm elated to know my father wanted me around. That he wanted more time with me. Yet whenever I visited, time with him one-on-one seemed scarce and impossible. It's completely different than my life with my mother. Here, I'm an only child. I'm a strong Black woman who needs no one."

Holiday scoffed and Tori snorted. I bit back a chuckle at the varying levels of irritation on their faces.

"And at your dad's?" Holiday asked.

"I'm Italian. No, a *Ricci*. Everything I do reflects the family and the standards and expectations that come with being a Ricci. I'm one of many, and privacy and silence go out the window."

Curse of the big families. But we wouldn't have it any other way, would we?

Once more, Noah's voice echoed in my head. Had I ever looked at the Ricci side of the family and felt like one of them? Appreciated their boisterous manner and the way they tried to include everyone?

"Why do you have to separate the two?" Tori asked. "Why not be both Octavia the strong Black woman *and* the Italian Ricci?"

I bit my lip. "I'm not sure how to be both. It's one of the reasons I love being a Christian—the chance to drop all labels and just be a child of God."

"Makes perfect sense to me." Holiday crossed her legs then flopped onto her back. "I have a song I've written that says something similar. It's not finished though."

"Everyone loves to label us. It's the American way." Tori rolled her eyes. "I've been labeled exotic for my eyes because, apparently, African Americans should only have dark-colored eyes. I've been categorized a 'Bell,' and the world certainly won't stop trying to put me in a box."

"But we don't have to live in it," Holiday objected. "I refuse to let someone stifle me because they're trying to figure out how I fit in the grand scheme of things. And when you think about it, every Christian is a puzzle piece and the Church is the entire puzzle. No two pieces look the same, so don't let someone's need to label make you feel like you can't be both Black and Italian."

"Amen." Tori clapped.

I giggled. "You guys are so good for my self-esteem."

"We've got your back, Tavia, just like you have ours." Holiday reached out and squeezed my hand.

"Thanks, ladies."

I stared at the wall, unseeing, before focusing on their faces. "When should we head out there? My dad said he'll send a jet."

"Fox has already been looking at his schedule to see when we can break away."

"Oh no!" I gasped sitting up straight. "What will his grandmother and niece do?"

"They're used to spending the holidays without Fox."

"No, I can't have that. Invite them along as well."

Tori's eyebrows rose. "Are you sure?"

"Positive. I'm sure my father won't object. He has enough room." At least, I hoped he wouldn't object. But Tori and Holiday were my family, and since Tori had just married into the Fox family, I couldn't expect her to leave them.

"I'll let Fox know."

"Great. Are you and Emmett good, Hol?"

"Yes. He's excited." A wistful smile creased her face.

"Looks like you are too."

"I am. I can't wait until the wedding."

"Did you settle on a venue?" Tori asked.

"We're having it in Napa. I already called the church we went to when we vacationed there last summer."

My heart melted. "You two are so cute." Holiday and Emmett would live a wonderful, long life together.

I want that, Lord. Now that I didn't have ballet to occupy my time, loneliness filled its place. Striving for perfection, for the dream of ballet, had left me without anyone to share my accomplishments with. Sure, I had my family and friends, but no one who was just mine. It was hard to see what the price of my dream truly was.

At the end of the day, Tori would leave to be with Fox, and Holiday had Emmett. Even my mother had a life, which she'd put on pause to come help me. I knew she was seeing someone, even though she hadn't mentioned his name or introduced me to him. But I'd caught the cutesy laugh she'd cut short when I hobbled into the room while she was on the phone. I hadn't asked yet, but I would. Eventually.

"So, a June Napa wedding?" Tori asked.

"Yes. Does it sound crazy?"

"Not at all." Tori shook her head.

"Sounds like perfection, Hol." I smiled at her. "You're going to be a beautiful bride."

"And you two will be great bridesmaids." She rubbed her hands with glee. "I've got some dresses I think could work."

"What colors did you pick?"

"Navy and gray."

"That's so you. I can't believe you're going to be my sister-in-law next year." Tori shook Holiday's arm and then squealed. "I can't stand the excitement."

Their laughter covered my sigh. A bum knee and solo status was just what I needed to feel less than. "Hey, guys, I think I'm going to take a nap."

Holiday sat up. "Are you okay?"

"Just tired. Headache." All true, but the pounding in my head had nothing on the ache in my heart.

"Alrighty. Do you want something for the headache?" Tori asked, coming to a stand.

"No. I think the nap will take care of it."

"If you're sure."

"I am. Thanks." I shifted slowly to lie on my side, propping a pillow between my legs to help elevate my knee.

"Talk to you later. I'll text you what Fox says," Tori said.

"Thank you." I waited until I heard the click of the door to let the tears flow freely.

Why does this hurt so much, Lord? Why am I so envious of my friends? Please, please take this ache away.

I didn't know much about relationships, but it didn't take a genius to figure out that if I entered a state of desperation, I could end up doing something foolish. Something like think of a dreamy green-eyed doctor and how I didn't feel so alone when he was around.

How being around him brought a calm and peace I didn't feel away from him.

Starting anything with the good doctor was pure foolishness, and I was no fool. My mother had raised me to be cautious and mindful of not doing something I would regret.

Lord, help me.

My phone chimed, and I sniffed back tears. The notification showed I had a text—from Noah.

N: Something came up and I need to reschedule our meeting tomorrow. Could I come later in the afternoon?

What had happened? I wanted to ask but didn't want to poke my nose where it didn't belong either.

O: That's fine. Not like I'm going anywhere.

N: What? No hockey games to attend?

I chuckled through the tears and wiped my face.

O: Not tomorrow. Maybe next week.

N: Ha! Living that box life.

O: I'm not Sam-I-Am.

N: Boo. Nerd joke.

O: I thought since it was a bookish one, it was right up your alley.

Noah sent me a GIF of Robert Downey Jr. rolling his eyes.

N: I needed that laugh. Thank you.

O: I hope everything is okay.

N: Me too. See you tomorrow at one?

O: That's fine.

He sent a GIF of a puppy waving with the word *goodbye* scrolling along on the bottom.

And just like that, my heart felt lighter. My worries not so big. All because of a doctor that I couldn't erase from my mind.

I PRESSED THE BUTTON ON THE SIDE OF THE RECLINER, AND THE footrest rose slowly to an extended position. My leg seemed to sigh with gratitude as I leaned back.

"Comfortable?" Holiday asked me from her own recliner.

"Perfect."

"Good. Maybe you should get some rest?"

I eyed her, wondering why she was acting all concerned. I was doing much better on crutches now. "I'm fine. Enjoy your fiancé."

Holiday nodded hesitantly then turned toward Emmett.

I studied my father's jet. There was rich and then there was Ricci Rich. The cream leather interior gave a hint of his wealth, but in case I or anyone using his private jet had any doubt about the level of the Riccis' net worth, the guest bedroom in the back would be the clincher. I'd slept on the downy, soft king bed the first hour, but my stomach had demanded I come and find provisions.

"Thank you," I murmured as the flight attendant placed a plate of sliced fresh fruit before me. I nibbled quietly as Emmett and Holiday whispered to one another.

Thankfully, they were situated on the other side of the

plane, but I was very aware of their bubble of romance. Tori hadn't been able to come with us to Tuscany. Fox couldn't maneuver his schedule enough to fly out of the country, so they'd opted to make it a New York Christmas.

And worse, Tori had decided to move fully into Fox's home. I'd known it was coming, just hoped it would be more gradual. Now the fourth floor was empty. Holiday and I had tried brainstorming ideas on what to do with the space, but so far, we couldn't agree on any of our ideas. What was the point when Holiday would probably move in with Emmett or find another home with him once they married? I would be the lone woman in a huge townhouse all by myself.

I picked up my cell and scrolled through social media—thank goodness the jet's Wi-Fi was better than a commercial flight. None of the notifications caught my interest. A text notification pinged, and I smiled as Noah's face flashed on my screen. He'd given me permission to take a picture of him at my last treatment session.

N: MERRY CHRISTMAS EVE. ENJOY ITALY.

O: MERRY CHRISTMAS EVE TO YOU TOO. ARE YOU STAYING IN THE CITY?

N: WE ARE. GOING TO MY GRANDPARENTS'
TONIGHT FOR A FAMILY DINNER.

O: AWESOME. WE'RE IN THE AIR AND THEN WE'LL HAVE DINNER AT MY FATHER'S.

N: ARE YOU NERVOUS?

O: YES.

N: YOUR DAD'S PROBABLY NERVOUS AS WELL.

I hadn't thought of that. And now that I knew my father had always wanted me around, maybe this wouldn't be so bad.

O: YOU'RE RIGHT. THANK YOU FOR THAT PERSPECTIVE SHIFT.

N: HAPPY TO HELP. YOU DESERVE A GOOD CHRISTMAS.

O: SO DO YOU.

I smiled at the winking emoji he sent.

"What are you smiling about?"

Holiday stared at me expectantly as I met her gaze. "Uh, just a text."

"A text from who?" she sing-songed.

And the bad thing about the teasing note in her voice? Holiday was a professional singer, so even when she wanted to be annoying, she sounded good.

I sighed. "From Noah."

"Oh, Dr. Swoony-Swoon?"

A chuckle erupted despite my burning face. "You and your nicknames. And you need to stop peering below the surface."

"Why? 'Fraid I'll see how much you like him?"

My eyes darted to Emmett.

"Hey." He put his hands up. "I'm not here." He pulled some ear buds out of his pocket, slid them into his cell phone, and closed his eyes.

Holiday got up and sat in the recliner directly across from me. "So, what's going on with you two?"

"Nothing. We just text occasionally."

"About what?"

"Nothing. Anything."

Holiday's brown eyes roamed my face. "You like him."

"I can't." I drew in a shaky breath. "He's my doctor."

"Like you can't get another one."

But I didn't want to. I looked forward to seeing Noah three times a week. The thought of him not coming, not bringing light into my darkness…well, tears sprang to my eyes, and I battled them back. "It's not that simple, Hol."

"Still trying to live by other people's expectations?"

"Holiday, I'm not like you. I can't meet adversity head on like you or Tori. If I even get a whiff of something negative coming my way, I want to do a one-eighty and run."

"I'm not buying that. How else did you become a principal ballerina? That has hardship written all over it."

"And look what I'm left with now." The words ripped from my throat. I made a deliberate effort to release the tension in my body as I became aware of the death grip I had on my cell. "I don't know who I am without ballet. I'm just trying to take my recovery one day at a time to keep the darkness at bay."

"Tavia." Holiday's bottom lip trembled. "I'm not trying to hurt you. I just want you to see that Noah could be another dream."

I blinked. "What do you mean?"

"No one said to give up on ballet. On dancing again. I'm saying maybe open your heart to see if Noah could be another dream. You can have more than one, you know. It's okay to want ballet *and* to be with someone who gets you. Loves you because of who you are. Makes your life richer." She glanced over at Emmett, and a soft smile curved her lips.

A relationship wasn't a dream I'd dared to have. And the few times entering into one had crossed my mind, I'd quickly batted the desire away. "Noah would make life too complicated."

"Or he'd make it better."

"I don't know, Hol."

"In my opinion, you should open that door, because it looks like he's knocking." She nodded toward my phone, which had another notification from Noah. She rose to her feet. "Think about it. Seriously consider it." Then she crossed the plane and resumed her place by Emmett, leaving me to my thoughts.

N: THANK YOU. I'M LOOKING FORWARD TO THE FOOD THE MOST.

I stared at the words he'd written. As much as Holiday urged me to consider him a possibility, I just couldn't bear to lose his friendship and the brightness he brought to my life. To change that status quo could have me ending up like my mother—without a partner to do life with.

I'd rather be miserable all by myself than brokenhearted and alone.

O: THE FOOD'S MY FAVORITE PART AS WELL. WHAT DOES YOUR FAMILY COOK?

I gave myself a mental pat on the back for sounding like everything was okay on my part.

N: MY GRAN MAKES DRESSING, CRANBERRY SALAD, AND THE BIGGEST TURKEY SHE CAN FIND. WHAT ABOUT YOUR FAMILY?

O: WELL FOR LA VIGILIA (CHRISTMAS EVE), ITALIANS TRADITIONALLY EAT SEAFOOD AND VEGETABLES TO PREPARE FOR THE GRAND MEAL ON CHRISTMAS DAY. AT LEAST THAT'S WHAT MY FATHER TOLD ME. HE DIDN'T WANT ME TO BE SHOCKED THAT THE MEAL ISN'T LIKE AN AMERICAN ONE. MY MOM ALWAYS COOKED A NORMAL-SIZED MEAL SINCE IT WAS JUST THE TWO OF US.

N: REALLY? SO WHAT KIND OF SEAFOOD? DID HE TELL YOU?

It was the same question I had asked.

O: HE DID. THERE WILL BE SHELLFISH, REGULAR FISH, AND AN ASSORTMENT OF ROASTED AND BASTED VEGGIES.

N: SEND ME A PIC IF YOU GET A CHANCE.

O: OKAY. YOU TOO.

I sighed. Sending pictures and greetings was something friends did, right? I could no longer claim that our relationship was strictly professional. I didn't have any other doctors in my contact list. Wait, not true. My primary care doctor was, but the number was to her office, not her personal cell.

I closed my eyes, willing my thoughts to cease pounding against my feelings. Leaning back in my seat, I blew out a breath and prayed for sleep to come.

❧ 14 ❧

HOLIDAY GASPED AS WE PULLED UP TO MY FATHER'S TUSCAN villa. The warm-yellow stucco home reached toward the blue sky. A three-tiered fountain beckoned from the center of the circular cobblestone driveway. Our driver stopped the car, and Ernesto, my father's right-hand man, opened the door, helping Holiday out before Emmett had a chance to.

She turned around and motioned to me. "Give me your crutches."

I passed them to her before Ernesto offered his hand to help me from the car. "Grazie, Ernesto."

"*Buon pomeriggio, Signorina* Ricci."

"Good afternoon to you too." I gestured to Holiday. "This is my friend Holiday and her fiancé, Emmett."

"Nice to meet you," he said as he shook both of their hands.

Ernesto had been working for my father for as long as I could remember. He'd always been the one to pick me up from the airport when I was a kid or greet me at the door in my adulthood.

"*Dov'è* mio babbo?" I blinked. How easily I'd slipped into Italian.

"He is in his study. He had a phone call to finish but will be out as soon as possible."

Of course. Business first. I hid my disappointment and thanked Ernesto.

He motioned for us to follow him. "I will get your bags later."

"Grazie," Holiday chirped. She stared at me as if asking *was that right?*

I dipped my head and offered a reassuring smile. She'd been looking up Italian phrases since I'd asked her to come. Ernesto opened the heavy black wrought iron door and we filed in. Familiarity washed over me as I stepped atop the burnished orange tiles in the foyer. Conversation greeted my ears, most likely coming from the kitchen. Then again, if the family was here, people could be all over the villa.

A slight tapping noise echoed across the floors, and then he appeared. My father. The man who'd apparently wanted me in his life more than I had ever realized—or dared hope.

"Piccolina!"

"Babbo." I sniffed back tears as he wrapped his arms around me.

The faint smell of cigar clung to his clothes as he rubbed my back.

"*Come ti senti?*" he whispered.

How *did* I feel? Tired, from the flight. Happy, because I was getting my first Christmas with my father. Sad, for the state of my relationship with my mother. Heartbroken, because I was still on crutches and couldn't see the light at the end of the tunnel.

"I'm fine, Babbo."

He pulled back, his brown eyes assessing me from his lined face. At sixty, my father looked every bit his age. His skin was as tanned as always from time spent outside caring for his babies—the grapes that were his livelihood—but white

85

hairs had infiltrated his black locks, giving him a more salt than pepper style.

"You are not."

I shrugged. "Let me introduce you to my friends."

"We will talk later," he murmured.

"Sí, Babbo." I motioned for Holiday to come closer. "This is my friend, Holiday Brown."

He engulfed Holiday's hand between his two. "Welcome, welcome. I have heard so much about you."

"Likewise." She smiled at him. "And this is my fiancé, Emmett Bell."

"W. Emmett Bell?" My father's bushy eyebrows rose.

"Yes, sir."

"Wow." Babbo looked down at me. "You know some important people, piccolina."

"No more than you."

"We Riccis know how to make friends, yes?"

"I think Holiday picked me. Not the other way around."

"No, we picked each other." She reached out, and we squeezed one another's hands.

"I'm glad she's had you for a friend all these years. I do love that she does not live alone in the city, you know?"

"Definitely. We can't be too careful."

"Exactly. The city can be dangerous. Look what happened to your friend Tori."

I shuddered at the memory of the stalker and the damage he'd wreaked.

"I've always wanted her to take care. Be safe," my father continued.

"I am, Babbo."

"Bene, bene." He clapped his hands together. "Come. Let us go. The rest of the family is here and waiting."

At his proclamation, my stomach jumped as if a troupe of ballerinas had started performing out of sync—mass confusion in a jumble of moves I couldn't begin to label. Did the rest of the family want me here? Had they also wished they could know me a little better? I didn't keep in touch as well as I should. But didn't that work both ways?

We followed him into the dining area, and a chorus of ciaos and *salve*s greeted us. My stepmother stepped forward, looking cool and elegant in a cream-colored jumpsuit. Her brown hair hung down to her waist, beautiful threads of silver hinting at her age, just five years younger than my father.

"Ciao, Octavia." She kissed me on my left cheek then my right. "How was the jet?"

"Very comfortable. Thank you for sending it."

"Oh, that was your father." Lines fanned out from her brown eyes and framed her mouth. Although her hair wasn't as gray as my father's, her wrinkles were keeping up with his.

I made another round of introductions, then we searched for empty seats.

"Piccolina, sit here." My father gestured to the seat next to the end of the table, where he always sat.

"Grazie, Babbo."

He placed my crutches against the wall and clapped his hand together. "Nothing brings me greater pleasure than to see my family here. Octavia, welcome, welcome." He looked toward my brother, who sat across from me with his wife. "Don, your mother and I are thankful you are never far away. And Bianca, just a short drive or quick flight and *presto,* you are here."

His eyes reddened as he looked around the large dining table. My grandmother was seated at the opposite end on the same side as Holiday, Emmett, and I sat. Tomorrow, the rest of the extended family would join the festivities.

"Now, let me pray."

I was surprised to hear him pray in English, but he probably assumed Holiday and Emmett didn't speak Italian—which they didn't. They would have been lost if he'd said grace like he usually did. My heart softened toward the man I had spent so much time resenting and loving all in one breath. Thank goodness I could take today and the remainder of my visit to enjoy him and our relationship.

As plates were passed around, I filled mine, taking in the noise and chaos that came with this family. But I also tried to look at it with different eyes. As one who belonged and wasn't the odd duck. Granted, having Holiday and Emmett helped. For once I wasn't the only brown face at the table. I didn't feel so strange in my father's home.

But then my gaze would clash with Paulina, and feelings of inadequacy would rise once more. I didn't know why my stepmother had never warmed to me. I could only assume it was because I was a reminder that my father had been married once before. Had loved someone else. Had another child. I didn't allow her to live in an illusion of one love to last a lifetime. Granted, they'd been married longer than my parents had been—longer than Don and Bianca had been alive.

"Ignore her," Holiday whispered from my right.

"You'd think I'd be used to it by now."

Holiday snorted. "If anyone got used to not being liked, pity on them."

"So you agree? She doesn't like me?" I whispered out the corner of my mouth.

"It's early yet, but she sure isn't putting out any warm fuzzies."

I sighed.

"Piccolina?"

"Yes, Babbo?" I met my father's gaze.

"When will you be all better?"

"I was told to expect at least six months of therapy before

looking at dancing again. And even then, I may not be back to principal status."

His brow furrowed, reminding me of a hound dog. His raspy voice deepened. "You get second opinion?"

"I trust my doctor, but I did ask some others who had been in similar situations."

"Any of them principals?"

"Two were."

"Were, hmm?"

"Well, now you can settle down." Bianca smiled. Her long brown hair fell in elegant waves. She was practically a carbon copy of Paulina, but a lot younger and more friendly. "Being married with a child, it's a blessing. Are you dating?"

"No."

"That's okay. I know plenty of single men." She tilted her head as if running a mental Rolodex of men she knew. "I know. I will have Paolo come tomorrow."

"No." Don curled his lip, giving him an edgier look than the five o'clock shadow clinging to his face. "Paolo is not faithful. Why not Giovanni?"

I watched in amusement as my half-siblings bickered back and forth. I didn't have the heart to tell them I would never date an Italian. I'd give Noah a chance before compounding issues and dating a man an ocean away. That would *never* work.

"Never say never," Holiday whispered.

"Are you a mind reader?"

She chuckled. "The look on your face says it all. But you actually muttered Noah's name."

"I did?"

"Told you you like him."

I rolled my eyes and snapped a picture of my food and a couple of discreet shots of the table lined with the fish and veggie platters.

"Going to text Noah?" Holiday teased.

"Hol?"

"Yes?"

"Shut up."

She threw her head back and laughed, then stuffed an oyster in her mouth and focused her attention on Emmett the rest of the meal.

🎄 15 🎄

CHRISTMASTIME IN ITALIA FILLED MY HEART WITH ALL THINGS magical. White lights decorated the streets and evergreen trees throughout town. I scooted along in the powered chair my father had ordered so I didn't have to navigate the cobbled streets via crutches. He said we would be doing much more walking than we Americans were used to.

I'd giggled at his comment, but now that we were almost to the end of viewing the offerings at the Christmas market, I was thankful for the mobility scooter. I had only taken the time to stand when something caught my eye. Like now.

Bianca sidled up to me. "*Bellissima.*" She gestured to the snow globe I held in my hand.

"Very." I stared at the Venetian glass in the snow globe shaped like a snowman.

"You will buy, yes?"

"I will." I smiled at Bianca. She had been taking the time to talk to me and get to know me better this trip. Granted, our rooms were right next to each other, so that might have something to do with it, too.

"I called my friend and mentioned you." Her eyes twinkled with merriment.

My stomach twisted. "You didn't. I don't want to be set up."

"Why not? We were not made to be alone. Marriage," she sighed, her grin tilting wide. "The best thing there is in the world."

"If you end up with the right man, perhaps." But how could anyone be certain of that?

Bianca motioned toward her husband a few booths away. "I actually did not want to marry. I am young and did not want to settle down, but Marco, he did not stop pursuing me. There came a point when I could no longer deny my feelings. Now I feel foolish for waiting so long."

She was only twenty-four. How long could he have pursued her? "How long have you two known each other?"

"Since primary school."

"When did you start dating?"

Bianca smiled. "When I turned twenty-one."

Huh. "Do you two have a lot in common?"

"No, but that does not prevent us from spending time together. When you love wholeheartedly, you will move mountains for your spouse." She linked her arm in mine. "You know this feeling?"

I didn't. But after being around my roommates, I certainly wanted to experience it. "I'm not sure I'm ready for dating."

"Ah, you must have someone in mind then. You are scared, yes?"

I wanted to say no, but that would be a lie. "Yes," I sighed.

"I will pray for you to be as fierce in love as you are on the stage."

I giggled. "I don't think anyone has described my dancing that way before."

"Oh, but it is. When you do those jumps and then let your partner swing you around..." She shuddered. "I would be petrified. I have always admired your dancing."

"You have?"

"Yes."

I bit my lip. "Why have we never been close? Never talked on the phone or anything else sisterly?" Was that even the way to say it?

Bianca shrugged. "I was self-absorbed until I began dating him. Then I felt like it was too late." She pulled her arm away and looked me in the eyes. "Is it?"

"No."

"Bene. Then we will talk on the phone and do all the sisterly things, yes?"

I smiled. "Yes."

I WANDERED DOWN THE HALL, SEARCHING FOR A PLACE OF QUIET. As much as I was enjoying my holiday, the noise was a bit much, and I desperately needed some moments alone. But there wasn't a rooftop here for me to escape to and decompress. Hence my mindless wanderings through the expansive villa.

I stopped in front of the library door and cracked it open in order to peek and see if the room was occupied. Empty. A rush of air fell from my lips as I pushed the door wide and hobbled in. Finally, I would get some peace and quiet. After quickly shutting the door behind me, I made my way to the sectional in front of the floor-to-ceiling shelving that filled one wall. I didn't need to pick up a book, just wanted to soak in the silence the closed door had secured.

My eyes closed in relief as I leaned against the couch cushions, legs spread before me on the chaise end of the sectional. I visualized barre exercises. Imagined the foot movements of the *battement tendu.* How my foot would be in fifth position and my body free from pain but muscles taut with exertion.

Would I get there again? Would I be able to evoke muscle

memory as my body strived to express the artistry of ballet? I sighed. My dream of returning to the stage seemed so elusive.

The words Holiday had spoken on the plane came to me. I could have two dreams. One didn't have to replace the other. But the dream of having a family seemed just as unattainable.

Noah.

On the surface, Noah seemed like the kind of guy a girl would love to get to know better. But I didn't want my children to have to deal with the trials of my childhood—the struggles to fit in and know how to identify myself. And if I let Noah know I was interested—assuming he even returned that interest—would I be able to go forward despite my concerns about the drama that could spring forth?

The door clicked, and my eyes flew open.

I sat up. "Hello, Babbo."

"What are you doing all alone, piccolina?"

"I needed some quiet time."

"Ah. You are like me. Too much noise and your head feels like it will explode, yes?"

"Sì." Not that I didn't enjoy seeing my nephew terrorize my brother with his antics.

Donnie kept bringing the outside in. He'd brought me a rock the other day and given his mother a lizard he'd managed to catch. I was amazed how she took it in stride and even smiled at her son before shuddering and throwing the reptile right back outside.

My father sat down on the other end of the sectional. "How are you enjoying your visit?"

"It's been nice. Bianca and I have been talking more." *Like I wish you and I would.* Yet the words I longed to say to my father stuck in my throat.

"You should visit more."

"And you should come to New York more." I bit my lip. Hadn't meant to say that. But really, why did I always have to be the one extending the olive branch?

"This is true." He rubbed his hands down his khakis. "I have not been a very good father, have I?"

"I wouldn't say that."

"But you would not say I *have* been a good father, no?"

I gulped. "I've always wanted a closer relationship with you. But the miles between us make it seem impossible, Babbo."

A deep sigh filled the room. "You are right. It does seem impossible at times. But this I know. You are my daughter. My firstborn. I will do everything in my power to be a better father. To close the gap. Like now. I sent the jet. This brings us closer, yes?"

I smiled. "It does."

"And I have the FaceTime. We never use this."

"We could try. When I go back, I mean." I stared down unseeingly. Should I bring up past holidays? Hear his side of the story?

"We will do more than try. We will talk. Once a week?"

"That sounds good."

He studied me, a contemplative expression on his face. "You are not going to ask?"

"Ask what?"

He wiped a hand down his face. "Your mother told me what you discussed. How you are upset with her."

"And you're not?" A shock wave vibrated through my body.

"I have forgiven long ago. Back then I certainly was angry. Seems like I have always been angry with your mother for some reason or another. Oil and water, we are."

The thought saddened me. How I'd wished my parents could have made it work, but he hadn't wasted time finding another woman. "She kept me from you."

"She did. But it was not all her fault."

My eyes widened. "How can you say that?"

"Paulina," he sighed. "She wanted me to focus on the children she and I made, and the fight kind of"—he made a *pfft* noise—"gone. Surrounded by strong-willed women, I gave in to both of their demands." He met my gaze. "*Mi dispiace,* piccolina. I should have fought harder. Should not have given up on seeing you more. Should not have given in to them. I am sorry."

My head dropped back onto the cushion. I didn't know what to say. I wished *I forgive you* would fall from my lips, but right now hurt bruised my heart.

"Octavia, will you forgive me?"

The brokenness in my father's voice shattered my hurt pride. "Always, Babbo."

He wrapped his arms around me, and I placed my head on his chest. "*Ti amo.*"

"Ti amo, Babbo."

❧ 16 ❧

A WEEK LATER, I BLEW OUT A STEADY BREATH AS I SANK INTO A squat.

"You're doing great," Noah encouraged.

"It doesn't feel like I am."

"You are. Remember how you felt after surgery? You could barely bend your knee."

I pursed my lips. "But I'm still not where I want to be." Could only maintain a squat at about a sixty-degree angle.

"That's because you're impatient." He winked.

Heat skittered through my limbs. Since I'd returned to the city, I'd had a harder time pushing my growing interest in this man away. Somehow, Noah Wright had gotten under my skin.

"I'm not impatient. Just driven."

"By impatience."

A chuckle tore free before I could hide it.

Noah stopped his pacing. "Time."

I took my time straightening, feeling his gaze on me.

"Octavia, you've got this. You're going to dance again."

"Yes, but at what level?"

"The level God wants you to."

My shoulders slumped as I leaned against the wall. How could I rebut that logic? "You're right."

"But you don't want me to be?"

"It's not that."

He motioned for me to sit. "Then what is it?" He folded his arms as he leaned against the end table while I sank onto the exam table.

A brief moment of déjà vu filled me as I remembered Noah's stance and need to talk from before. Somehow my physical therapy appointments had become mental health sessions. Talking to Noah was so easy and drained the stress of this whole ordeal from me.

"I want to be a principal again. But what if God says no? Then what will I do?"

"Step into the call that He has for you just as elegantly as you've done in your pointe shoes."

My mouth dropped open. He sounded so confident. "How do you know though? I haven't done anything else *but* ballet."

"Sure you have. You've been an A student. A daughter, a best friend, and I'm sure a mentor to countless other ballerina hopefuls. I'm sure you've been an accountant and social media manager as well."

"May-be." I drew out each syllable.

He chuckled and that groove appeared in his cheek. I wanted to reach out and touch it. See if that slight stubble he kept on his face would prick against my skin or be smooth.

Mamma mia! It was hot in here. I gulped and averted my gaze to his shoes.

"You'll handle whatever comes your way, and remember that God equips the called. So whatever He has in store for you, you either already know how to do it or you'll learn."

"Then I'm praying for joining the company as a principal again. It's what I know." What my heart yearned for.

"But you're not incapable of learning other things, Octavia."

"I don't know about that, *Noah*."

His eyes twinkled. "You're such a pistol."

"What?" I giggled. "You say the strangest things."

"Says the ballerina with mish-mash of Italian and New Yorker accent."

"Oh no. I sound perfectly normal."

"To your ears."

I tilted my head. "And to your ears?"

"I enjoy listening to you speak." His face took on a redder complexion.

His shyness shouldn't get to me, but it did. Made me want to push just a little to see if he had all these unresolved feelings like I did. If he didn't, I'd be embarrassed and grossly disappointed.

But if he does?

I didn't know what I'd do with that information, so I maintained the status quo. A few jokes here and there, and longing glances kept to a minimum. Although, I was pretty sure I'd reached a new level today.

"I want to try something new next time," Noah announced.

"What's that?"

"Pool therapy."

I blinked. "Come again?"

Noah smiled in amusement, his green eyes twinkling with suppressed laughter. "I want you to come to a pool I use for therapy. Give your knee a good workout without any added pressure."

"I don't think that's a good idea."

"Why not?"

Because water terrified me. I'd rather skydive than put myself in a pool. I didn't even take baths. But admitting that, being vulnerable…

"I just can't."

"Can you not swim?"

Sure, I could admit to that. Lots of grown women couldn't swim, right? "No."

"That's not a problem. I won't make you swim. Think of it more like water aerobics."

Eh. Still did *not* want to get into a pool. "How about we do something else?"

"Octavia?"

I met Noah's steady gaze. "Yes?"

"I'll be right there with you." His scrutiny pierced me, jumping my heart into overdrive. "I won't let anything happen to you. I won't put you in a situation you can't handle."

But he was. Making my heart want things I knew weren't good ideas. Making me believe that some issues could be overcome.

"I don't know," I whispered.

He reached out, taking my hands in his. I barely bit back a gasp as warmth coursed through me.

"I won't let anything happen to you. You'll be safe, and your body will get a better workout. Get you steps closer to being a principal again."

"But in a pool? Really, Noah?"

"Trust me."

My hands tightened around his before reason set in and I let go. Noah didn't know what he was asking. "Can I think about it?"

"Yes. If you decide to take the plunge, no pun intended, text me. I'll let you know where to show up. If not, I'll be here Friday."

"Okay."

He studied me. "Do you want to talk about it?"

"No."

"Okay then." He gave a slow nod then stood. "Let's

finish up."

By the time I'd been through the rest of my therapy routine, exhaustion pulled at me. I crutched my way to the stairs to say goodbye.

Noah turned to look at me over his shoulder. "Don't forget to think about it."

"I won't."

"You sure?"

"Positive."

"Bye, Octavia."

"Bye," I whispered. I turned away so I wouldn't be tempted to watch him until he was out of sight. Unfortunately, my mother stood before me. "Mom."

"Octavia, are we going to talk now?"

I gulped. Every day, I'd been praying for God to help me forgive. Every day, silence reigned supreme and the distance between us seemed to widen. Maybe this was one of those times I knew the right thing to do and God was just waiting for my obedience. "Okay."

Relief filled my mom's face, softening the hard lines that had made her seem almost angry.

"Tavi, I need you to know how sorry I am."

"I know, Mom."

She rested her hands on my shoulders. "Do you?"

"Yes," I sighed. "But that doesn't lessen the hurt. I've spent years believing I wasn't wanted. That he didn't mind the distance between us. And now I find out the one person who was supposed to have my back caused that divide? How would you feel if you were in my shoes?"

Tears spilled over my mother's cheeks. "Awful."

"I'm not trying to hurt you, but I need to figure out a way to forgive you and not feel so much bitterness and anguish every time I see you."

"Maybe it's time for me to go back to my place."

I bit my lip. I didn't want her thinking I was banishing her, but a little space might be best. "I'll let you make that decision."

Her shoulders straightened. "Then I'll return home. I'll check on you in a few days."

"Thank you." I wasn't sure what I was grateful for. Her care or her leaving. Or both.

"I love you, Octavia."

I held in a sigh. "I know."

She dipped her head and brushed past me.

I did a mental assessment, but the only feelings I could sort out were hurt and anger. *Please help me forgive and bridge our relationship, Lord. Please talk to me.*

But I still felt nothing.

❧ 17 ❧

MY LUNGS WORKED IN STACCATO BEATS AS I GRIPPED NOAH'S hands.

"Breathe. I've got you."

"I…am," I rasped between inhales.

"Not very well. You're going to hyperventilate if you keep that up."

Well, if he would stop pulling me farther into the pool, I would be able to keep my intakes of oxygen from spazzing out. But I couldn't say that. It took more effort to formulate words than to continue with my shaky inhales and exhales.

"Octavia, look at me." Noah spoke in a stern voice.

My eyes immediately snapped to his. "What?"

"Where's your favorite place in the whole world?"

I didn't even have to think about that one. "Being on stage."

"Eh." He shook his head. "Try again."

My lips twitched. "I don't know."

"Sure you do." His thumbs rubbed the backs of my hands as if trying to coax a deeper answer from me.

Goosebumps broke out along my arms. "The rooftop of our house."

"Why?"

"Because I go early in the morning. When the city is still practically asleep. The sounds are faint, but still there. And the skyline is magnificent when the sun breaks through the horizon. It's where I feel God the most."

"Do you listen to music when you're up there?"

"Sometimes."

"Instrumental or with lyrics?"

I smiled. "Depends on my mood."

"If you could listen to your favorite song—one with lyrics, that is—what would you pick? And please, not an Italian song."

I laughed out loud. "What if my favorite song is Italian?"

"Too bad. Pick an English one. Maybe even one you sang all the time in high school."

"High school, huh?"

"Yes. What did you listen to?"

"Well, I was a huge Bruno Mars fan. Holiday and Tori too."

"All right." He gave a slow nod as if he was thinking. "I want you to do a *plié*."

"No!" My eyes widened. "The water will rise."

"It's not even above your waist—and you're short, so that's saying something."

My gaze skittered down to check the water level and then back up to Noah's face. He looked so calm and steady. Like standing in water was an everyday occurrence. Something natural. I'm sorry, but God gave me legs, not fins.

"Don't tense back up on me now. You were doing fine."

I exhaled. "Why do you want me to bend?"

"One, it's an exercise. Two, I'm going to try something."

"Fine." I rolled my eyes and slowly bent into the move.

"Good girl. Now do ten of them."

As my body sank into the movement again, Noah started singing. I froze, mid *plié*, and listened as he sang the first lines of "Count on Me" by Bruno Mars. He squeezed my hand, and I rose to first position before dipping again.

As Noah sang about friends being there for one another, my body relaxed, forgetting its location in the death trap known as a pool. Because my mind wasn't on counting how many *pliés* I'd done, I couldn't even get nervous about the sound of lapping water. No, I was mesmerized by the man serenading me so I wouldn't freak out.

And even though the lyrics talked of friends, this moment felt like so much more than that. His voice trailed off and I watched the movement in his throat, fascinated by his display of nerves.

"How do your leg and knee feel?" His voice came out a little hoarse.

All I could feel was the hammering of my heart against my ribs. "Noah," I whispered. I couldn't believe he had sung for me. To ease my fears.

"Yes?" He stepped closer.

"I…" I what?

He took another step closer. "You?"

"I…" I rose on my tiptoes, lessening the space between us as I rested my hands on his shoulders.

"You…" His breath fanned out, caressing my lips, and my eyes fluttered shut as I closed the gap. His lips were soft, fitting perfectly against mine. His hands gripped my waist as he took over the kiss.

This.

My hormones did a *chaîné* of pirouettes as I slowly sank onto my heels. We pulled apart simultaneously, and I couldn't help but think my face must have had the same look of wonderment that covered Noah's.

I'd kissed Noah.

Noah had kissed me.

We'd kissed.

"Oct-tavia, I…"

I stepped back. "Should we end this session early?" My mouth dried out as I wondered what he wanted to say. Did he wish to apologize? Beg forgiveness? Or—ask me on a date? I bit my lip, feeling how plump it had become.

"Yes. We should." He cleared his throat. "I don't want you to overdo it."

I nodded, taking the hand he offered so he could lead me out of the pool. He passed me a towel, and I wrapped it around my middle, doing my very best to ignore him. But it was like King Kong had decided to sit between us, head turning back and forth waiting for one of us to point out his existence.

After slipping on my flip flops, I headed to the dressing room. I quickly changed then sank onto the bench. How could I go out there? Face him? Look him in the eye? I had no idea what to say. What to do.

It would be dumb for me to say I didn't like him. I'd kissed him, for goodness' sake. But that didn't erase the hesitant feelings I'd been harboring. I still thought dating him was a bad idea. Only now I had his kiss to replay in my mind to persuade me otherwise.

I fingered the edge of my T-shirt. Sitting in the women's locker room forever wasn't an option. Mac would be by to pick me up in—I checked the time on my cell phone—ten minutes. But if I did hide away that long, would Noah leave? Go to another appointment?

"Octavia, you can't hide in there forever."

A giggle rose unwittingly. "Why not?" I called out.

"Because we need to talk."

"That's a dreaded phrase."

"Don't make me come in there."

"Fine. Calm down." I grabbed my bag and walked out. I was down to one crutch now and couldn't wait until I could walk without aid.

Noah stood by the ladies' restroom, already changed and

still adorable. My gaze dropped to his mouth, and the memory of his lips teased my senses.

"Octavia," he growled.

I startled, eyes meeting his. "What did I do?"

"You can't just stare at my mouth like that."

I bit my lip.

"Or do that to yours. I'm not a monk."

"And all this time I've ben thinking, 'well, the good doctor surely is a monk among men.'"

He rolled his eyes, dragging his hand through his hair, then began to pace. "The kiss."

Was spectacular. I bit back a dreamy sigh. It was time to get real. To remember why we couldn't work. "Was just that. A kiss."

He halted, his mouth dropping wide like a fly trap. "Are you kidding me right now?"

"No." I would never forget that kiss.

"You can't just call it a mere kiss. That wasn't just *a kiss*." He used air quotes, and I had to keep from giggling at the incredulous expression on his face.

A flustered Noah Wright was an adorable Noah Wright. The pulse in my neck jumped. I wasn't going to make it out of the pool house unscathed, was I?

He stepped forward, the toes of his shoes touching mine. "I know I crossed a line, and I fully intend to set up a colleague of mine to take over your physical therapy."

"What? No!" I gripped his arm. "I don't want anyone else." I grimaced inwardly at the double entendre.

"I can't be your doctor with this"—his hand waved between us—"chemistry, feelings, whatever between us."

"Do you want me to apologize? Because technically, I was the one who kissed you." I beat back the tears watering my eyes. "I'm sorry. I won't do it again."

"But what if I want you to?"

I gulped, hearing the noise as loudly as the alarm that woke me every morning.

"I like you, Octavia. A lot." His green eyes searched mine. "How do you feel about me?"

Oh no. He'd asked. He voiced *it*. "I…"

"You…?"

"Please don't start that again."

A strained chuckled fell from his lips, but I focused on his eyes. Looking at his mouth had gotten me in trouble last time.

"I would love to take you out on a date." Noah touched my arm lightly.

I squeezed my eyes shut. "I can't, Noah."

"Why? I can find you another physical therapist."

"It's not about that."

"Then what? Talk to me," he pleaded.

"I don't date."

"At all?" He straightened as if the thought had never occurred to him. "Surely you've dated before."

"A few times, but no, not really." And I couldn't with him.

"Because of ballet?"

Among other things. But I simply nodded.

"And you don't think you can be in a romantic relationship and be a ballerina?"

"I've never wanted to in the past."

He paused. "You're not dancing right now."

"But I will." *I had to!* "It's not fair to you to start something that I have no intention of finishing."

"And the finish line of dating?"

"Marriage."

"I see."

"Do you?" Would he accept my answer? Or dig deeper?

He slid his hands into his jean pockets. "Have you ever dated a white guy, Octavia?"

My head jerked back. How had he gotten so close to the heart of one of my fears? "What does that matter?"

His jaw ticked. "Please just answer the question."

"No," I whispered.

"Is that a problem for you?"

"Not dating a white guy?" My heart rate accelerated as he got closer and closer to the truth.

"No. Is my race—the fact that I'm not Black—a problem for you?"

"I'm half—"

"Answer the question, Octavia," he pleaded.

If he had shouted or yelled, I would have ignored him. But the hint of urgency in his voice undid me. "Yes." I closed my eyes. "In my experience, interracial relationships just don't work."

"Says who? Your parents?"

"They're a prime example." I opened my eyes only to see a hang-dog expression on his face. It chipped at the hardness surrounding my heart.

"So you're going to ignore all the other examples that say otherwise."

"I don't know those stories."

"Then we need to change that."

My phone chimed with a text, probably from Mac saying he was here. "I have to go."

"Okay."

"Will I see you for my next appointment?"

Noah ran a hand through his hair. "Yes," he gritted out.

"Thank you."

He nodded, squeezing his eyes shut as if my gratitude pained him. Taking another look, I catalogued his features, then left him standing all alone.

❧ 18 ❧

My thumbs flew over the cell phone keypad, thumping away on the digital device almost as fast as my heart beat inside my chest.

O: SOS. Be home stat.

T: On my way

H: Here and waiting. Do we need ice cream?

I considered Holiday's question. I had no idea.

O: Undetermined.

H: Have food apps up and waiting.

A chuckle flew from my lips. Part relief that my friends would rally behind me and give me much needed advice, and part humor. Holiday loved food and knew all the best places to eat or order from in the city. If I could figure out the feelings rumbling around in my insides, then I could tell her what to order.

But I was a jumbled-up mess. As if a bunch of tiny ballerinas were doing *sautés* in my stomach. Sure, they were light on their feet, but a lot of repetitive jumping was sure to make anyone nauseous. It wasn't the motion going on in my stomach but Dr. Swoony-swoon—as Holiday called him— who was all to blame.

And in light of that magnificent kiss, worthy of the nickname. A sigh expelled from my chest as my fingers rose to touch my lips. We had kissed. How could I see him at my next appointment and act like nothing had happened? What had I been thinking?

I squeezed my eyes shut only for them to fly open as the passenger door opened.

"You're home, Ms. Ricci."

"Thank you, Mac." I took his proffered hand and rose. "Have a good evening."

"You too."

I'd barely made it inside when Holiday rushed toward me. "What happened? Are you hurt? Are you okay?"

"I'll tell you when Tori gets here. I'm not hurt. And being okay is debatable."

Holiday huffed. "As long as you're not hurt. I can't handle any more injuries."

So true. Her fiancé had been shot by Tori's stalker. Tori's husband—and former bodyguard—had been shot as well. And I…well…Tori's stalker had upended my life with one attack. But I wasn't going to focus on that.

"How far away is Tori?"

"I'm right here."

I turned as she waved her key in the air. "Still have a key."

"Of course you do," Holiday exclaimed.

"We'd never make you give it back." I returned her hug. "I'm so glad you two are here."

"What's the SOS?" Tori asked, her blue-green eyes assessing.

I peered at Tori then Holiday and let loose my thoughts. "I kissed Noah."

"What?" they cried.

"Are we celebrating this or upset?" Holiday asked, scrolling through her phone.

"What are you doing? Pay attention," Tori snapped.

"I'm ordering food appropriate for the mood." Holiday looked at us as if we should have already known this fact.

I shook my head. "I'm not sure. The kiss was amazing but shouldn't have happened."

"So, carbs?" Holiday asked.

I giggled. "That'll work."

Tori smiled in bemusement. "Should we move into the kitchen so you can sit?" She eyed me on the crutch.

"Yes, please."

We walked into the kitchen, and I blew out a breath, trying to figure out how much to tell my friends. I wouldn't go into the details of the kiss. Of how amazing Noah's lips had felt against mine. My face burned with the memory.

"Sit and spill," Holiday demanded as she dropped into the chair next to me.

"All the details," Tori added, taking the seat on the other side of me.

"He took me to the pool—"

"Wait a minute." Holiday held up a hand. "You willingly got in water?"

"Craziness, huh?"

"Unbelievable is more like it," Tori said.

"He promised I could trust him and that he wouldn't let anything happen. But I was petrified."

"Gotta love phobias," Holiday muttered.

"Okay, so you two were in the water," Tori prodded.

"Right, and we were holding hands. More like I had a death grip on his as he kept trying to tug me farther in. He could tell I was close to losing it, so he started asking me all these questions about music."

"Why?" Confusion covered Holiday's face.

"Hush, girl. Let her finish." Tori propped her chin on her hand.

"So he could sing to me."

The girls' mouths both dropped open.

"He sang Bruno Mars' 'Count on Me' and told me to do one of my exercises."

Holiday's hand flew to her chest and literal tears filled her eyes.

"Oh my goodness, Tavia. If that didn't melt you…" Tori shook her head in wonder.

"Right? I was stunned, and the next thing I knew, I kissed him."

"Did he kiss you back?" Holiday demanded.

"Yes," I sighed.

"Ohhh," the girls intoned.

My face was already warm with the memory, but it was heating more now from embarrassment as they gave me knowing looks.

"Good kiss?" Tori asked.

"The best."

"But?" Holiday asked gently.

"He's white."

"Octavia," they said. Holiday's came out in a whisper, but Tori's came out in admonishment.

"I know," I groaned, dropping my head into my hands. "But guys…" I sighed, sitting up. "My parents—their relationship was volatile my entire childhood. You would have thought getting a divorce so early would have made it better, but every time the summer rolled around, both of their tempers would fly. Not to mention I had to grow up wondering how I fit in. My mom always telling me I was a strong Black woman and my dad telling me how I was a proud Italian."

"But Noah's an American. Don't you think that makes a difference?" Holiday asked.

"It definitely removes the strain international relationships cause, but people will see me and see him—a Black woman and a white man. You know there's a double standard. People barely bat an eye when a Black man dates a white woman, but the other way around?" I shook my head. "I just want to live in peace."

"But if you're avoiding someone for the sake of 'peace,' isn't that a lie?" Holiday's question echoed in my head.

Was it false peace to ignore a man who made my heart feel all the emotions? Safety, trust, amusement, and excitement?

"Life has already been hard for me, trying to become a principal at the same time as being Black."

"I know that, sweetie." Tori reached out and squeezed my hand. "I know what it's like to be scrutinized by the public and have every facet of your life under the microscope. But regardless of who you date, they're going to speculate."

"It's so true," Holiday joined in. "I don't know how many *baby bump* headlines I've seen since Emmett and I started dating."

"Yeah, but you're not going to get the *sellout* headlines, because Emmett's Black."

"Just because others compare shades doesn't mean we have to. Or live by their demands. Do you like Noah?"

I bit my lip. "Yes."

"Then why not go out on a date? See what happens. Nothing is set in stone, Octavia." Holiday smiled, probably to make sure I knew she wasn't trying to be harsh. Just offering the advice I'd asked for.

"I agree with Holiday. You genuinely like him. And that expression you had just now, remembering that kiss? I haven't seen you look that happy since your last performance."

"He said he wouldn't be my therapist if we dated."

"He asked you out?" the girls asked in unison.

I chuckled. "Yes. But I don't want another doctor."

"Is there a rule saying he can't work with you? He's a physical therapist not a mental health professional."

"True." But still. It was kind of weird. "I don't know."

"Have you prayed about it?" Holiday asked tentatively.

I shook my head.

"Then that's what you should do." She held out her hand, palm up. "Let's pray now."

"Okay."

I held hands with the best friends God had ever given me and we prayed. Prayed for wisdom, prayed for me to break free of other people's expectations, prayed for healing in my body, heart, and soul. It was one of the best prayers I'd heard, and for a moment, a *tiny* moment, I felt God's presence.

❧ 19 ❧

THE NEXT MORNING, I AWOKE TO THE CHIME CHIRPING ON MY cell phone. I frowned, staring at the alarm app. *Eight o'clock.* Had I hit snooze? Sitting up, I unlocked my phone and checked the notification. Noah had sent a text. I opened it and stared in bemusement.

N: 17 YEARS OF HAPPINESS.

He'd attached a link to his statement. I clicked on it and read the headline. It was about Mildred and Richard Loving, the couple who had fought against the law that made interracial marriages in Virginia illegal and had convinced the Supreme Court to rule the edict unconstitutional. Apparently, they'd had seventeen blissful years together before Richard passed away.

What was Noah trying to say? I wasn't sure what to reply.

O: WILL YOU BE HERE TOMORROW?

N: UNTIL YOU TELL ME OTHERWISE.

O: WHY WOULD I TELL YOU NOT TO COME?

N: BECAUSE

O: BECAUSE WHAT?

N: BECAUSE YOU'LL SAY YES TO THAT DATE.

I bit my lip. I could admit I liked him, but could I let go of the fear that a relationship between us was doomed for failure? Jump in with both feet and expect him to catch me?

O: So if I agreed to a date, you'd stop being my physical therapist?

N: Seems the ethical thing to do.

O: What if I don't want anyone else but you?

Nerves erupted in my stomach. Why had I hit send so fast? Being around Noah Wright gave me too many moments to gaffe.

N: Then go out with me.

N: Please.

O: I need to think and pray about it some more.

N: Okay. I'll add my prayers to yours.

O: Prayers that I'll say yes?

N: Of course ;)

I giggled. He certainly was honest. I reached for my Bible on my nightstand and opened the page where my bookmark lay. Each year I made it a goal to read the Bible in its entirety, always changing how I did so. Whether it be chronologically, a little each from the Old and New Testament, et cetera. Thankfully, there were a number of apps and ways to keep track. Today's reading had me in Proverbs 10. Verse 12 stopped me in my tracks.

"Hatred stirs up strife, but love covers all sins."

No mistaking the hatred that was the core of racism. I'd faced my fair share as I fought for my place in the ballet world against those who held to ideals that ballerinas could only look a certain way. My brown skin certainly broke that mold. And in Italy, I'd always been met by surprise at the fluency with which I spoke the language. When my father introduced me to his associates as his daughter, there was always a pause on first meeting.

But my father loved me and had never presented me as if ashamed of my racial makeup. How had I missed that? How had I let the bitterness of being in New York while he lived his life in Italia blind me to the ways he showed his love to me?

My mind drifted to Noah. To his plea that I go out with him. If I did date and eventually fall in love with him, could that see us through difficult times? Would we have more good days than bad? We didn't live in the time of the Lovings, but racism still existed. It pervaded America's past and seeped into its present, from internment camps for Japanese Americans during WWII to the hatred of Muslims after 9/11, the attacks against Asian Americans during the COVID-19 pandemic, and more.

But if this city had taught me one thing, it was that we could also celebrate those different cultures. You could order food on every corner. Yucca fritas from Bolivia next door to Cantonese steamed dimsums. But still we seemed to stick to our own culture instead of intermingling in other areas of life.

Lord, show me how love can bridge this gap. Am I viewing my parents' relationship the wrong way? Please drop the scales from my eyes and replace them with Your truth. May I learn to see as You see. Amen.

I closed my Bible and rose to ready for the day. Noah wouldn't be here today, but I still had to do my exercises so I could get back to dancing shape. *Principal* shape.

As I threw on my clothes for the day, the verse from earlier repeated in my mind with an image of my mother. She loved me. Had always loved me. I couldn't imagine the heartache she must have felt losing me every summer. Especially since we were together the rest of the year. How had she felt, being alone for Christmas? Imagining me enjoying the festivities with my father and half-siblings?

I had to forgive her. Restore our relationship to what it had been before. I reached for my phone and clicked her number before I could talk myself out of it.

"Tavi, sweetie, how are you?"

"I'm okay." I sat down on the stool in front of my vanity.

"Are you?"

Are we? The question remained unspoken, but I heard it loud and clear.

"I love you, Mom. I'll always love you." I swallowed. "I forgive you."

Sniffling reached my ears. "I'm so sorry. I don't deserve your forgiveness."

"But you have it, because I love you."

"Thank you, sweetie." Her voice trembled.

"Please stop crying."

She sniffed again. "Okay."

"Do you want to go out later? Do something?"

"Is your knee okay?"

It was extra stiff this morning, and judging from the weather app on my phone, I could guess why. "I'll take some pain meds if we go out and then more when we come back… if it's time."

"Are you sure?"

"Yes."

"Okay. Let's have lunch."

"Perfect." I opened my mouth to ask her about Noah, then shut it. I wasn't ready for motherly advice, especially since I didn't know which direction she'd lean.

Would she agree with my belief that interracial relationships were nothing but heartache? Or would she tell me to make my own choices? Learn from my own mistakes?

I bit back a sigh. "See you soon."

"Bye, Tavi."

After doing my rehab exercises, I walked back into my closet and traded my yoga pants and ballet shirt for dark-wash skinny jeans and a tunic. A scarf completed my ensemble. I was ready to enjoy time with my mom as if nothing bad had happened.

❧ 20 ❧

NOAH WAS COMING. I'D ALMOST DRESSED UP FOR THE OCCASION, and had to force myself to put on workout shorts and a T-shirt. Still, I was tempted to let my hair down and throw on some makeup. Utterly ridiculous considering all the times he'd seen me bare faced.

But this time was different. He'd sent a text of another interracial couple this morning—this time of Seretse Khama and his British wife, Ruth. They had remained married until his death.

Not only was Noah sending me interracial couples who had influenced history with their marriages but ones who'd remained together until death. Was he trying to tell me he was interested in something more significant than dating? Or was I just reading too much into his links?

I swallowed and walked into my studio, nerves tight like a live wire. Footfalls sounded on the stairs, but I focused my eyes outside the ballet studio window. If I turned now, I might melt at the sight of him. Say yes if he asked me to date when I hadn't felt an answer from God just yet. Then again, I hadn't felt any presence from Him other than when I had prayed with Tori and Holiday. Was it possible He'd spoken without me realizing it?

"Octavia?" Noah's warm voice flowed over me like melted wax.

I inhaled a shaky breath and turned. Oh man, he looked more adorable than I remembered. His brown hair was in disarray. Now that I knew how his hair felt between my fingers—silky and smooth—it would be harder than ever to resist touching.

"You can't stare at me like that, remember?"

My eyes shot down to his face. Had I held a dreamy expression over just his hair? "Right. I remember."

His lips curved in a half-grin. "Do you?"

I remembered a whole lot more than that. "Yes." My lips twitched as I held my smile back. "I'm ready for today's session."

"Did you get my text this morning?" He stepped forward.

I nodded.

"And?"

"I'm still thinking."

"You take a long time, don't you?" He walked toward me.

"Do you want me to rush and make a hasty decision?" I tilted my head as I studied him.

"Well, yeah, I *am* a guy who's interested in getting to know you on a personal level. But no, because I want to know you've said yes because you know it's the right thing to do." He stopped moving, standing before me.

"Is dating you the right thing?"

He trailed a finger down my cheek. "What do you think?"

Yes. I wanted to fall into his arms and let him chase my cares away. But as much as I wanted to, I couldn't. Not yet at least. I respected Noah too much to just say yes because my hormones wanted to feel that electric spark his lips brought.

"I'll let you know when I figure that out."

He nodded. "Fair enough." His hand fell to his side.

Noah walked me through the exercises that I'd done in past sessions before introducing something new. As I walked with a band around my legs and moved side to side, he studied me.

"Want to go to the pool again? Was that okay?"

Heat flushed through me as I remembered our kiss. Now every time I got in a pool I would be thinking of the firmness of his touch. The sweetness of him singing to me. The gentleness in his kiss.

I gulped. "It was fine," I squeaked.

"So next session, a pool one? Whether it's me taking you or an associate?"

"I'm not going in a pool again unless it's with you."

His green eyes twinkled. "You make it really hard for me to be mad at you."

I stopped side stepping. "Why would you be mad?"

"Because I want to take you on a date." He stepped forward. "Show you what being with me will be like. But when you tell me that you only want me to run your physical therapy, only want me in the pool with you…" He sighed. "I can't be mad."

"What if you dated me *and* remained my doctor?" I searched his eyes, holding my breath as I waited for his answer.

"Are you saying you'll go out with me?" His hands trailed down my arms, then his fingers intertwined with mine.

"I'm leaning toward it."

"What if I only do pool sessions with you?"

"That would be ideal."

"And I could let someone else handle your PT sessions?"

I nodded, unsure of what I was agreeing to.

"Then Octavia Ricci, will you go out with me?"

I stared into Noah's warm green eyes. Let warmth course

through me as his thumbs drew lazy circles on the backs of my hands. Being with him felt right. I just needed to take a chance.

"Yes."

His eyes closed and he placed his forehead against mine. "Thank God. I owe Him."

I chuckled. "Hold your thanks. We could go out, and then you may decide you're just not that into me."

"I sincerely doubt it." He brushed his lips against my forehead. "I know we haven't finished our session, but I don't trust myself." He stepped back. "I'm going to go."

"Now?" I bit my lip.

"For temptation's sake."

"What if we went into the living room or kitchen?" I didn't want him to go. "I'm sure Holiday is around here somewhere. We could have a chaperone."

"No." He shook his head. "Maybe later on, but I'm going to go home and plan our date."

"Are you?" I grinned.

"I am. Can I pick you up tonight at seven?"

My eyebrows rose. "Tonight?"

"It is Friday."

"You don't want to wait until next week?"

He growled low in his throat and tugged me close again. "Tonight. Seven. I'll pick you up."

"I'll be ready," I whispered.

He brushed a kiss against my cheek and walked backward, maintaining eye contact. "I'll let you know who'll be handling your sessions from now on."

"But not pool therapy."

His lips tilted. "The pool is ours." He disappeared around the doorway.

I fanned my face. Who knew talking about a pool could overheat the senses? I bit back a squeal. *I had a date with Noah*

Wright! I hurried to my room and grabbed my cell. The girls would be happy to hear this news and, hopefully, help me figure out what to wear. I couldn't remember the last time I'd been on a date.

O: I SAID YES.

H: TO A DATE?

T: WHEN?

O: JUST NOW.

H: WHEN'S THE DATE?

O: TONIGHT

T: SOMEONE'S IMPATIENT

H: HOW ROMANTIC!!!

The line of emojis accompanying Holiday's exclamation points had me cracking up.

T: WHAT ARE YOU GOING TO WEAR?

H: WHERE ARE YOU GOING?

O: I HAVE NO IDEA.

O: TO EITHER

O: THAT'S WHERE YOU TWO COME IN.

T: ANOTHER SOS?

O: IF YOU NEED ME TO SAY YES SO FOX LETS YOU OUT OF HIS PRESENCE, THEN... SOS!

Holiday sent a GIF of a baby laughing and falling over. I snickered and sent one of a person laughing as they covered their mouth.

T: I'LL BE THERE SOON! DON'T START THE FUN WITHOUT ME.

H: NEVER! BUT I'M COMING UP THERE TO LOOK THROUGH YOUR CLOSET.

T: I CAN GET YOU AN OUTFIT IF YOUR CLOTHES ARE OUTDATED.

H: DOES SHE OWN ANYTHING BESIDES BALLET TEES AND YOGA

PANTS?

I snorted. Probably not. Well, besides the outfit I wore to lunch with my mother. I did have a bunch of sports jerseys as well.

O: I HAVE OTHER CLOTHES.

T: JERSEYS DON'T COUNT.

O: DRAT. HOW DID YOU KNOW?

H: LIKE WE HAVEN'T SEEN YOUR
OUTFITS BEFORE. IF YOU'RE NOT
IN A TUTU, YOU'RE WEARING YOGA
PANTS.

It was a sad truth. But I had learned to dress up when I was out on the town with them.

O: SHOULD WE GO SHOPPING?

H: LET ME FINISH CLIMBING THESE STAIRS.

Holiday huffed as she rounded the corner and entered my bedroom. "Surely you have clothes in here that don't look abysmal."

"I don't know. Never thought about it. I just grab something I can be seen in next to you and Tori."

She pushed back hanger after hanger. There really was no rhyme or reason to how I hung my clothes. Wherever I saw open space, an item went in that slot. I wasn't sure why I didn't have a system. Probably because my mother had always organized my closets growing up, so I'd rebelled when I moved out. Now I was used to the chaotic disorder. There was sense to my mess, at least to me.

"You don't have a black dress?"

"Sure I do." I pulled the requested item from the corner and handed it to Holiday.

"Pass. Do you have a different one?"

I pulled out one with a longer hem line.

"Ugh. Looks like something your grandma should wear."

"Thanks," I stated wryly.

"You're welcome." She beamed and pushed more hangers aside, muttering under her breath.

The sound of boots pounded on the stairs before a breathless Tori entered the closet. "I made it," she huffed.

I giggled. "You haven't missed anything. Just Holiday accusing me of dressing like my grandmother."

"You don't all the time. Just ninety percent."

I shook my head, taking their teasing in stride. "Obviously Noah doesn't care how I dress. He asked me out when I looked like this." I gestured toward my workout clothes.

"But you're so pretty it really doesn't matter what you wear," Tori said.

"It's because she's so short and petite. Guys are a sucker for short girls."

"Not all guys," Tori said dreamily.

"Newlyweds," I muttered.

Holiday chuckled. "Did you bring any outfits with you, Tor?"

"Yeah, I laid them on the bed."

We left my closet as Tori showed us her choices. "I got this for a photo shoot, but the hemline barely crossed my bottom, so I never wore it." She placed the red dress on the bed. "It might look good with some tights and ankle boots."

"Meh."

She held up a jumpsuit. "The designer got my size wrong. I can't fit into this, and she told me to take it and sell it."

The black one-piece was kind of cute. "Maybe."

"Last but not least, a plaid skirt. I figured you'd have a top you could wear with it."

I looked at the black skirt with white plaid lines running through it. "I like that one." I bit my lip, thinking of the clothes in my closet. "I could wear this with my white turtleneck."

The girls clapped their hands in approval after I grabbed my long-sleeve top and showed them.

"Perfect," they chimed.

"We'll help with makeup, so get showered." Holiday made a moving motion with her hands.

"All right, all right." I stepped into my bathroom then looked back at my friends. "You guys are the best."

AT SEVEN O'CLOCK, THE DOORBELL RANG. TORI HAD LEFT A HALF hour ago, and Holiday was waiting for Emmett to come get her in thirty minutes. For some reason, she'd felt the urge to take pictures of Noah and me as if we were prom-bound teenagers. I'd had to beg her to go to her room so that I could meet him on my own—with a promise we'd take date selfies.

A full troupe of ballerinas had once again taken up residence in my middle. I felt slightly nauseous as I unlocked the door for Noah, but one look at him and those feelings were replaced with lightheadedness that had my head swimming.

He wore a black V-neck sweater that peeked out from his open peacoat. "Wow, you look amazing." His voice held a slight rasp, and shivers went up my spine.

"So do you."

He made a twirling motion with his finger, so I did a one-eighty, thankful I'd chosen flats instead of the knee-high boots I'd wanted to wear. I wasn't confident enough with my knee yet to try walking in shoes that had any kind of lift. I paused, facing Noah once more.

He stepped forward and cupped my face. "Is it bad to kiss before the first date even starts?"

I couldn't prevent the grin that stretched across my face. "Only if your date objects."

His eyes searched mine and he lowered his head, lips hovering just above mine, our breaths mingling. "Do you?" he whispered.

"Not at all." I closed the gap between us, wrapping my arms around his neck.

My body came to life as he kept the kisses soft. He pulled back. "Are you ready to go?"

I nodded.

"Where's your coat?"

"Oh, right." I blinked through my kiss-induced haze. Where had I put it?

"Is that it on the banister?" Noah pointed behind me.

Yep. There was my coat. I grabbed it and the clutch I'd placed on top of the railing.

"Here," Noah said, appearing by my side. "Let me help you."

I slid my arms through the sleeves as he draped the coat over my shoulders. My face warmed with the attention. His fingers brushed my hand before they laced between mine. He led me out of the door and carefully down the steps.

"How's your knee feeling?"

"Good."

He nodded and opened the car door for me. I paused before getting in. "Where are we going?"

A lazy grinned slid onto his face. "You'll see." He closed the door behind me and rounded the front end to get in the driver's seat.

"No hint at all?" I asked after he buckled.

"Just enjoy yourself."

"Okay." I smiled. "I'll do that."

"I sincerely hope so."

As he drove to our mystery destination, the conversation flowed nonstop between us. He talked about the antics he'd gotten up to with his cousins. About how learning about God at a Christian camp he'd been wrangled into attending—his words, not mine—at the age of sixteen changed his life forever. His parents had apparently thought he'd been abducted by aliens and replaced with an obedient child.

I couldn't contain my giggles as he did voices to imitate his parents. They sounded like wonderful people. and I wondered what they—well his mom—thought about him going out with a Black woman. Part of me wanted to ask him, the other part just wanted to do like he said—enjoy the night.

"What about you? Any funny childhood stories?"

"I'm afraid I was kind of a serious child."

"I can see that. Dedicated ballerina with no time for fun."

"Something like that. Holiday and Tori were always pulling me out of my shell. All my funny memories involve them."

"Longtime friends are the best."

"Definitely. Do you have a best friend?" My nose scrunched. "Do guys say that?"

"No." He chuckled. "But my cousin you met at the hockey game—I'd call him my best friend if I had to label it."

"Having family for a best friend must be even better."

"I don't know. I mean, it makes it convenient to hang out, since we end up at all our family gatherings. But I've seen how much your friends care about you. I'm sure you three have created a bond as strong as family, maybe even stronger in some cases."

"True. I'm not that close to my half-siblings, but I would totally count Holiday and Tori as sisters."

"See?"

He pulled up to a nondescript brick building. There was no sign or anything giving a hint as to where we were.

I swallowed. "Um, are we here?"

"That we are." He threw the car into Park, and a man wearing a red vest opened my door.

"Are you here for the event?" he asked us.

"Yes, sir," Noah stated.

"Fantastic. Welcome."

I exited the car while Noah rounded the hood to come stand at my side. The valet gave him a ticket, and Noah led me up the steps.

"What event?" I whispered.

"We're at a pop-up."

My mouth dropped open. In all the time I'd lived in the city, I'd never gone to any pop-up events. Sure, I'd heard about the craze. Holiday and Tori had both gone to at least one, but for publicity purposes. I'd probably been at a rehearsal or ballet class each and every time they'd gone. How much of life had I missed by being so *dedicated?*

The doorman took our coats and gave us tickets to retrieve them at the end of the event. Noah slid the vouchers into his pants pocket then took my hand in his.

"Ready to have fun?"

"Yes. What kind of pop up is this?"

"Winter wonderland is the theme. It's got a maze set up, and the finish line opens to a restaurant. They'll serve food that fits the theme."

"Awesome. Oh, and I promised Holiday we'd take date selfies."

He looked bemused. "Date selfies?"

"Yes. It was that or have her treat us like we were going to prom." I grabbed my cell and swiped the screen so the camera would face us. "Say winter wonderland."

Noah placed his head against mine and we smiled. I snapped a few pictures and then locked my screen.

He led me into the room. Walls had been erected all around to create a maze. We entered the first walkway and I grinned. Fake snow littered the walking path, and snowflakes hung from the ceiling. At the end of the walkway was a station that held shopping sacks. The instructions read:

Take one to hold your winter wonderland keepsakes.

We grabbed one and turned down the corridor. Hanging from the ceiling at the end of the tunnel was the number one. *Ornament Station* hung below the number. Tables were lined against the walls, and other couples seemed to be building ornaments.

"Did they forget Christmas already happened?"

"Guess there's always next year."

I wondered where we'd be in a year. Would Noah have decided our relationship wasn't worth it? Would I? So far, we hadn't received any strange looks from passersby. No one had curled their nose or assumed we were there as singles.

"What are you going to put in yours?"

Noah's question brought me out of my thoughts. "Um…" I looked at the table and its offerings. There were little charms to add inside our ornaments and stoppers to plug them up.

"Snow?"

His chuckle warmed me. "Just snow?"

"All right, all right. Give me a moment to think." I scooped some snow to line the bottom of the orb. Then added a mini Statue of Liberty and a trinket with the year. What else could I add?

"Why those two?"

"That way I'll know where I was and when I made this."

"Smart."

"I need something to help me remember this as our first date."

Noah handed me the number one. "How about this?"

"Perfect." I smiled, my grin widening as he added one to his ornament as well.

He'd lined the bottom of his with snow as well, but the rest of his charms were different. He had a dancer, a heart, and the Empire State building.

"What's with the heart?" My mouth dried out as I waited for his response.

He just smiled, lines fanning out from the sides of his eyes. I broke eye contact and reached for the dancer charm and found one that had a stethoscope. It would remind me of the good doctor, wherever we may end up next year.

After we plugged our ornaments, we placed them in our bags and headed for the next station. It held the fixings for hot chocolate, giving us measurements for the cocoa base and how much of each topping we could add.

"Do you like Mexican hot chocolate?" Noah asked.

"What's in it?"

"Spices."

My nose crinkled. "I'll pass. I'm a lightweight when it comes to spicy food."

"Then what are you going to put in your hot chocolate?"

"Mint chips and marshmallows." My stomach rumbled as I added the ingredients to the dry powder. "What are you adding?"

"The red hots and marshmallows."

"Did you drink a lot of hot chocolate growing up?" I asked, peering up into his light-green eyes.

"I did. Especially during the winter. I'd come home from school, half frozen, and my mom would have a mug of hot chocolate waiting with some sort of baked goods."

"Like what?" We strolled to the next station, waiting our turn behind the couple in front of us.

"Chocolate chip cookies, pumpkin bread, scones, you name it. Whatever she'd been in the mood to bake."

"Wow. My mom is *not* a baker."

He chuckled. "I'm sure she has other talents."

She did. Her mind was like a steel trap when it came to organization. Probably why I was so messy now. Never had the opportunity to be so growing up. Good thing she didn't come to my place on a regular basis. I told Noah about my mom's neatness fetish, and he told me about his mom's comfortable philosophy.

"She believes if it doesn't make you comfortable, you shouldn't do it."

My eyebrows rose. "But some things *are* uncomfortable, and you have no choice but to do them."

"Come on. We all make choices. We can always choose another option."

True. It was why I was on a date with him. But was that wise? Was giving in to my feelings better than weighing them against others? Against the challenges I'd endured being a Black Italian?

"I don't know."

Noah laid a hand on my arm. "Listen. Choices can be uncomfortable, but if you know why you've decided to go a certain way, it makes all the difference in the world. Nothing better than knowing what you believe in, standing for what is right, and choosing to stick to those standards, no matter how uncomfortable it can become. Your comfort comes in knowing you're doing right."

"And how do you know what's right?"

"Pray. Weigh your feelings and thoughts against the Word. God always offers wisdom and peace."

"I like that you make everything seem so simple."

"When I know something, or someone, is worth it, it's very simple." He brushed his lips against my cheek and whispered in my ear. "Being with you isn't even a choice. It's a necessity."

"Noah," I whispered, before losing myself in his embrace.

❧ 22 ❧

THE MUSIC FUELED ME, ENCOURAGED ME TO STAND ERECT ON MY toes as my hands rose elegantly in the air. As Mark bowed, clutching my hand, I twirled, and Jacob took his place. Then Aaron, and finally Josh, as Prince Charming. I reveled in the beauty of placing my full weight on my left leg as my right did *piques* and helped me twirl into a pirouette.

Dressed in my tutu, I told the story of Sleeping Beauty for all who sat watching in the audience. I was no longer the daughter of Donovan Ricci. No longer the daughter of Angela Reese—my mom had quickly retaken her maiden name after the divorce. I was Octavia Ricci, principal dancer for the City Ballet Company. And, at the moment, I was Aurora.

A different song overlapped with the "Adagio"—Holiday's song "Brave." My lashes fluttered as I struggled to pull myself from my dream. Harsh reality greeted me as my eyes opened and sunlight flooded in. How long had I been sleeping?

I rolled over and grabbed my cell phone. Why was Holiday calling me?

"Hello?" I croaked.

"Are you seriously still sleeping?"

"Hmm. Guess so. What's wrong?"

"You're on the front page of the news."

I shot up. "What?"

"You and Noah are on the front page, looking quite content to snuggle in each other's arms. You didn't tell me he took you to the winter wonderland pop-up."

"You weren't home when I returned."

"Well, I'm home now. In the kitchen, eating breakfast and reading the article that's speculating who the handsome man is and how long you've been seeing him."

I groaned. "Why? They never talk about me unless it's about my dad or a performance."

"Oh, they threw your dad's name in here too."

"Great. That means he'll call me, because his publicist will flag it." I hated that my father's publicist had a social media alert for every time our names were linked together. Usually the publicity wasn't bad, because the papers usually only reported about my performances. But being linked to Noah— I didn't know *how* my dad would handle that.

"What's the picture look like?"

"Come downstairs and see."

"Fine," I muttered. I looked down, satisfied that my ballet pajama shirt was presentable enough. "No one else is down there, right?"

"Just me."

"I'll be right down." I grabbed my yoga pants and slid my feet into a pair of slippers. Since we didn't have company, I left my headscarf on—it kept my hair sleek and presentable while I slept.

After gingerly making it down the stairs and onto the first floor, I headed for the kitchen.

"Coffee's ready, and I had fresh blueberry muffins delivered."

"Perfect. Thank you." I smiled at Holiday.

"Sure."

She stood from the circular table with a paper in hand and tossed it onto the counter as I programed our espresso machine. There we were—Noah and I wrapped in each other's arms. Our lips prepped to kiss.

I sighed in relief. "They didn't get us kissing."

"Oh yes they did." Holiday flipped from the front page to one in the middle.

Oh! They'd caught the one of us right after Noah had claimed dating me a necessity. My cheeks heated at the memory. "Do you think it looks horribly sordid?"

"Not at all." Holiday smiled. "You look besotted in the first picture. The second one shows why." She snickered.

"Do you think he'll hate being in the papers?"

"I don't know." She shrugged. "But I'll be praying he doesn't freak out. Have you guys ever discussed ending up as a headline?"

"No," I whispered. Why hadn't I thought of that?

Probably because I was used to my name being linked to others by association, never someone else having their named linked to mine. As a ballerina, my name was always beside the company's. As Donovan Ricci's daughter, my name occasionally popped up in conjunction with his wineries.

"I should call him."

"Safe bet."

I sighed. "What am I going to do about him, Hol? Life just seems so complicated lately. I miss my routine. Miss the stability that being a ballerina brought me."

"Breathe, girl. Take it one day at a time. Stop looking at it as a whole."

"Isn't that short sighted?" I grabbed my cup and took a sip of the dark liquid. A sigh of satisfaction escaped as I swallowed the first soothing sip.

"No. Sometimes looking at what's ahead can bog us down with stress and anxiety. Plus, the Bible tells us not to worry about tomorrow. Just handle today, Tavia." She squeezed my hand then bit into a muffin.

"I'm surprised you're not eating a bagel."

"Already had one. But I was still hungry."

I shook my head. "Your eating habits are atrocious."

"Don't be jealous."

"I'll try not to be. I've been staring at the scales a little too hard lately. My body will have to get back in shape."

Holiday stared at me, eyes wide, mouth open. Her eyes scanned me from head to toe then stopped once more at my face. "Where did you gain weight?"

"Where *didn't I* should be the question."

"We'll add that to your worry about tomorrow list. Right now, you can only handle today."

"Well, I'm having a yogurt with this."

"Don't go crazy," Holiday mocked.

I giggled, thankful for the release of a little tension. "So…I need to call Noah."

"Yep." Holiday propped an elbow on the countertop and leaned her chin into her hand. "Can I listen?"

I shook my head. "No. I need some privacy." I pointed to our garden off the kitchen.

"Spoil sport."

"Go read your paper, Hol." I grabbed my cup of espresso and muffin.

After setting my items down, I took my cell out of my sweater pocket. Thank goodness I had grabbed it on the way downstairs. I bit my lip as my thumb hovered over Noah's name. *Just do it. Call him.* I pressed the icon and held the phone to my ear.

"Good morning, beautiful."

My face heated as delight fissured through me. "Good morning."

"How are you?"

"Well, um, I have something to tell you."

"Should I be sitting down?"

"Maybe?" I hated that my voice squeaked at the end, but tension coiled through me, making speaking difficult.

"Okay. I just sat on my couch. What's going on?"

"We made the front page of the papers."

"Which ones?"

"If I had to guess? All of them. But I've only seen one this morning. I haven't been on any social media sites to see how big it is." And maybe I should have before calling him.

"What does the picture look like?"

"Hold on." I hurried inside, snapped a picture of the two photos in the paper, then texted them to him. I sat back down in the chair outside. "I texted them to you."

"Yeah, my phone just chimed. Let me look."

I bit my lip as I waited for his verdict. Would he be angry? Decide this was a deal breaker?

"Wow."

Was that a good wow or a bad one? "What does that mean, exactly?" I asked hesitantly.

"It means I didn't realize how much you like me. Look at you."

My face burned with his suggestive comment, but I couldn't quite argue with him. I did like Noah. *A lot.*

"I'll have to cut these out and put them in a scrapbook."

"Seriously?"

"You don't like them?"

"We're plastered over the news."

"That's what happens when you have an interesting life people want to know about."

"Then you're not mad?"

"Not at all." There was a slight pause. "Wait, were you worried?"

I nodded then affirmed out loud.

"Tavia, I don't scare easily."

"Good." I exhaled the pent-up breath I'd been holding. "I'll see you later then?"

"I'm going out with my mom today. She loves antiquing. Would you like to have dinner tonight?"

"Yes, but my treat."

"Really?"

"Yes. Come over at seven?"

"I'll be there."

I hung up the phone and smiled. So far, so good.

EVERYTHING HAD BEEN PREPPED JUST IN TIME.

I removed my apron and headed for the front door. A quick look in the mirror in the foyer showed I still looked presentable. Yep. Makeup intact, hair curled behind my ears, and silk blouse flour free. I opened the front door to let Noah in.

"Hi." I peered up into his sage-green eyes.

"Hey." He leaned down, brushing his lips against my cheek.

My eyes fluttered close as I inhaled the scent uniquely him. Would it be too much if I buried myself in the crook of his neck, wound my arms around him, and never let go?

Noah straightened, and his lips quirked into a half grin. "Are you cooking?"

I nodded and pointed toward the kitchen. "The dough is all ready for us to make the gnocchi."

"You're making homemade pasta?" His eyebrows shot up.

"*We're* making homemade pasta." I pointed between us. "Are you impressed?"

"Very, but I thought gnocchi was made from potatoes."

"It is. I already cooked and turned the potatoes into the dough."

"Great. Let's do this." He clapped his hands together.

I giggled, covering my mouth then clearing my throat. "Let me take your coat."

He shrugged it off, and I hung the peacoat in the hall closet. I ran a hand down Noah's chest, loving the feel of his sweater. "This makes your eyes an incredible green color."

"That's why I wore it," he murmured, sliding his arms around my waist. "Had to look good for you."

Heat bloomed in my face, and I stepped backward. Being around him almost felt *too* good. I needed to remember to keep things light and far away from temptation. I grabbed his hand, tugging him to follow me. "Let's wash our hands. Once we prep the gnocchi, we'll make the soup."

"We're having gnocchi soup?"

"Actually, gnocchi clam chowder. You'll love it."

He rubbed his stomach. "I'm sure I will."

"Do you mind if we listen to music?"

"Not at all."

I hooked up my cell to the house's sound system, and Andrea Bocelli began streaming through the ceiling speakers. "All set."

"Great. Show me what to do." He gestured toward the island where I had the dough waiting.

I showed Noah how to roll the dough into knuckle-length sized pieces, then rub each chunk on the gnocchi board to get the signature lines the pasta was known for.

"We'll let those sit about 20 minutes." I pointed to the egg timer. "Could you set that?"

"Sure." He turned the dial. "What do we do in the meantime?"

"Get the clam chowder started. If you grab the pancetta out of the fridge, that would be great." I described what the

Italian meat looked like, and he passed that to me along with the butter.

"I'll chop and you cook?" I asked Noah.

"How about the other way around?"

I grinned. "Sounds great."

I browned the pancetta as he cut up the vegetables we'd add to the soup. We worked in a natural rhythm as I told him the ingredients we needed. The conversation that flowed in between put me at ease, but I was still very much aware of him.

I added clam juice to the pot as the veggies simmered, while Noah put the gnocchi in the boiling water after the egg timer chimed.

"How did you learn to cook?"

"I used to hang out in the kitchen at my dad's home whenever I visited. I felt awkward around my siblings." I sighed, leaning up against the counter. "And my stepmom never cared for me. I never had the guts to ask why, so my mind came up with all sorts of reasons."

"Like what?" Noah leaned against the empty counter tops across from me.

"Like, I was a reminder that he'd been married before. Loved someone before her."

Noah nodded. "Good guess. What else?"

"That she really was a wicked stepmother."

He chuckled.

I took a deep breath. "Or because I was half—"

He grimaced. "Did they ever say anything to make you think that?"

I nodded, looking down at the floor to avoid his gaze. Whether the comments had been born of curiosity or hate, I'd heard every one of them on the spectrum. Nothing had made me feel more different than the color of my skin. Not even being American had caused such heartache. Because hearing it from family was ten times worse than hatred from a stranger.

"I'm sorry, Octavia."

"It is what it is." I exhaled.

"Did your father have a cook?"

"Yes." I smiled, thinking of the jovial woman who'd taught me all about Italian cooking. "Signora Dagata took me under her wing. Showed me how to cook everything from breakfast to dessert. She never made me feel like a pest."

"Did you see her when you went back for Christmas?"

I slowly shook my head. "She passed away a couple of years ago."

"I'm sorry, Octavia."

"Thank you," I whispered. I turned and grabbed the remaining ingredients, hoping the busyness would keep the tears away.

Noah came to stand by me. "Thank you for sharing that with me."

My head bobbed vigorously as my lashes started fluttering with my obsessive blinking. But it wasn't working. Tears blurred my vision.

"Octavia…" Noah drew me into his arms.

I wrapped my arms around him and squeezed tight, inhaling as the heat of my tears saturated his sweater. Part of me was horrified. I never cried in front of people. *Never.* The other was so very relieved to have someone care for me. To soothe me as my feelings erupted.

After a few moments, I withdrew from the comfort of his arms. "I'm okay."

"You sure?"

"Yes." I grabbed a napkin and dabbed at my face, hoping I didn't have streaks of mascara or makeup on my cheeks. I peeked at the napery, which only had a few stains. "Be right back."

I hurried to the foyer mirror and examined my face. A few

touches here and there and I was once more satisfied with my look.

Noah's gaze assessed me when I walked back into the kitchen, as if to make sure I really was okay. Whatever he saw had him grinning. "Where should we eat?" He gestured to the kitchen table. "There? Or the bar stools?" He pointed to the other side of the island.

"Actually, if you don't mind the hike, how about the rooftop?" I had already turned on the patio heaters so that it would be nice and toasty when we went up there.

"That sounds great."

He cut up slices of bread as I ladled the soup into two bowls and then placed them on a tray. The rooftop had a wine fridge and glasses, so we didn't have to worry about carrying drinks as well.

Noah added the bread to the tray. "I can carry this up. You focus on the stairs."

"Yes, Doctor."

He smiled at the teasing.

As we climbed the stairs, Noah kept pace with me, furtive glances coming my way every so often.

"I'm okay."

"You sure?" At my nod, he continued. "I can run up the stairs and come back and carry you."

My body flushed with heat at the thought of being in his arms. "I'll be fine. I promise."

"I'm going to hurry anyway." He rushed up the spiral stairs and, before long, disappeared. Was he really going to carry me up the rest of the way? I'd come a long way from not being able to navigate the stairs to going up very slowly.

Still, the back of my thigh burned, and my knee wanted to groan in complaint. Footsteps pounded down the steps, and Noah reappeared at the fourth floor.

"You good?"

"Hamstring is burning, but I'll live."

"Then I'll assist." He swooped me into his arms.

"Noah, you don't have to do this."

"Please, you're so light. I feel like I'm carrying a ballerina."

I fought the chuckle as much as I fought the urge to bury my face in the crook of his neck. Before I could blink, he placed me down at the rooftop landing and took my hand in his.

"This is really amazing." He pointed toward the two heaters that stood sentry next to the outdoor table and chairs.

"I'm glad you think so." I lit a couple of candles situated in the center of the table that had been set for two. Noah had already placed the tray's contents on the place settings.

He pulled out my chair and gestured for me to sit. "Do you need to elevate your leg?"

"No. I'm fine. Please, tonight, no doctoring."

He nodded and sat in front of me. After offering to say grace, he bowed his head in prayer. I should have bent my head, but I couldn't resist the chance to study him. The reverent look on his face touched something in my spirit. I watched as he thanked God for all that we had and all that He provided, and it was like a warm blanket enveloped me. As if God had looked down on me and said *I'm here.* Tears sprang to my eyes, but I sniffed them back before saying, "Amen."

We spent the rest of the night getting to know each other over food. By the end of the night, I felt like God had been looking down on us with pleasure.

You're still here with me.

❧ 24 ❧

I did *not* like the new doctor. My feelings had nothing to do with the fact that he wasn't Noah Wright and everything to do with his horrible bedside manner.

Okay, maybe a smidgen of my dislike was due to missing Noah coaching and encouraging me to push through. But mostly, it was because the new PT was cold and unsympathetic.

"Ms. Ricci, you need to lower farther in your squat."

"I can't. It hurts too much."

"A little pain is good."

A little, yes. Fiery flames making me sweat with agony, no. I stood up. "I'm sorry. I can't do this. I tried to give you the benefit of the doubt, but no. Just no."

His ice blue eyes widened. "What's the problem?"

"You're not listening to me. I'm telling you I'm in pain, and you want me to push anyway."

"If you ever wish to return to the stage, then you need to motivate yourself through the burn."

This wasn't me being a prima donna. "Not to the detriment to my healing. Thank you for coming, but you can leave now."

His mouth opened. Shut. Opened once more. Yet no words came out. He inhaled and erupted. "Fine," he snapped. "See if I care."

He grabbed his gym bag, stuffing his items in while muttering under his breath. As he straightened, he gave me a cold stare. "See if I ever do a favor for Noah again."

"Oh, don't worry. I'll be sure to let him know what kind of service you provide to referred clients," I countered. *Jerk!*

He blustered, and I pointed a finger at the doorway. He could see himself out.

As soon as he vacated my studio, I sank onto the exam table, placing my head in my hands. Today's session had taken torture to a whole other level. My knee screamed. My thigh felt like it had taken a bite out of Hades. I just wanted to crawl into bed and remain there until the alarm woke me tomorrow morning. *So what's stopping you?*

I didn't have a job anymore. I didn't have to entertain my friends, once again finding myself all alone in our huge townhouse. I knew Noah had other patients to see. I really could just go crawl into bed and sink into my misery.

Which is where Tori found me a few hours later.

"What are you doing? Sleeping the day away?"

"My leg is on fire," I groaned. "And my knee won't stop throbbing."

Concern furrowed her brow. She placed the back of her hand against my forehead. "You're not warm."

"But I bet my thigh and knee are."

She slid the covers back and felt. "They are. Why didn't you get an ice pack?"

"I'm lucky I managed to make it to my bed."

"Did you tell Noah?"

"I didn't want to bother him. But you'll be happy to know I took an anti-inflammatory before crawling into bed."

"At least you're elevating it," Tori murmured.

"I barely remembered to do that."

"What happened?"

I told her about the new doctor and how much he'd pushed me.

Her frown deepened. "He sounds like a jerk."

I held up my thumb and pointer finger a millimeter apart.

Tori chuckled. "I'll get you an ice pack while you text your boyfriend."

I peered at her, feeling my eyes go wide. "Do you think he's my boyfriend?"

"Oh, sweetie, you haven't had that conversation yet?"

"No."

"You might want to. Especially if you're going to join the ranks of celebrities caught smooching."

I threw a throw pillow at her back as she left the room, cackling all the way. I tugged my cell phone off the nightstand and pulled up the last text conversation.

O: Hey, my leg is on fire and hot to the touch.

N: Are you serious? Did you hurt yourself?

O: No. Your doctor friend was just a little incessant in his demands.

Three dots appeared as I waited for Noah to type his thoughts. And waited. And waited.

N: What do you mean incessant?

Did he push you or hurt you?

Was he inappropriate in any way?

O: He just didn't listen when I said I was in pain. Told me it was necessary to get me back on stage.

He sent a GIF back of a man hulking with rage. I giggled, imagining Noah upset. He seemed so unflappable. Like nothing could fluster him.

N: I'll talk to him. Did you take any pain meds?

O: Anti-inflammatory

N: Do you have a fever?

O: No.

N: How long have you been elevating your leg?

I checked the time.

O: A few hours

N: I'm coming over. Let me finish with my current client.

O: You don't have to.

N: You don't want me to?

O: I didn't say that.

N: Good. See you soon.

Tori walked back in and handed me two gigantic ice packs wrapped in blue cloth casing. I placed one under my thigh and the other on my knee. "Thank you."

"Of course. Noah coming over?"

"After he finishes with a client." *Wait a minute.* I stared into her blue-green eyes. "What are you doing here? Did you leave something in the house?"

"No. I just wanted to see you and Holiday. Plus, Fox is working late today."

I knew there had to be a reason she would willingly pull herself away from her husband of a couple of months. "How's married life?"

"Wonderful." A full smile broke across her face.

It was no wonder she quickly rose to superstar fame in the modeling world. She was a beautiful woman, but being in love had taken her career to new heights. "And everything is going well with Sasha and Fox's grandmother?"

"Yeah, they're both great." She looked down at my bedspread. "I'm a little worried though."

"Why? What's wrong?" I focused on her, giving her my undivided attention.

"I think I'm pregnant."

I gasped. "Really?" I had to hold back my level of excitement at the look of worry on her face. "Are you not happy?"

"We've only been married for two months." Her brow furrowed. "We're still in the honeymoon phase. What if he hates the fact that a baby will come before our first anniversary?"

"He loves you. He won't be upset."

"What if I don't make a good mom?"

"Of course you will. You had a great example." Tori's parents were the best relationship icons in celebrity circles. "Have you taken a test?"

"Too scared."

"Did you at least buy one?"

She pulled three out of her handbag. I giggled at the absurdity of her walking through Manhattan with three pregnancy tests in her Coach purse.

"Where's Holiday? Tell her to get here stat so we can find out if you're pregnant or not."

Tori nodded and texted Holiday. Her phone chimed. "She's in her studio. She said give her five minutes."

"Do you need to drink some water?"

Tori laughed. "No. I'm good to go."

The suspense was killing me. I looked at the three boxes, comparing their success rating. "How late are you?"

"Two weeks."

I handed her a box. "Do this one. It's the best."

She opened and read the directions. Just as she finished, Holiday waltzed into my room. "What's up, ladies?"

"Tori thinks she's pregnant."

"Octavia's new doctor pushed her too hard."

We spoke fast and pointed a finger at one another. Holiday's mouth dropped open as her eyes jumped from my knee to the pregnancy test in Tori's hand. She let out a piercing scream, slapping a hand over her mouth.

I winced as my ear drums rang in protest.

Tori grimaced. "I don't know if I am yet."

"Well, what are you waiting for?" Holiday cried. "Go pee!"

I giggled and clapped my hands. "Get her, Hol."

Tori came out a few minutes later, a look of uncertainty on her face.

"Well?"

"Timer is set." She held up her iPhone. "When it goes off, I'll be able to read the results."

"How are you going to tell Fox if you are?" I asked.

"Yeah, a big reveal is definitely necessary," Holiday said. "Maybe even do something on social media for your Bexter fans."

While faking their engagement, Tori and Fox had their last names shipped as *Bex* by their fans, who called themselves Bexters.

"Can I find out if I am or not first?"

Her phone chirped. I slowly stood, and Holiday sprang to her feet.

"Where are you two going?"

"To look at the stick," we cried.

Tori shook her head but let us follow her. We stared down at the stick sitting on the counter, toilet tissue underneath for cleanliness' sake.

"You're pregnant," I whispered.

"I'm pregnant!" Tori exclaimed.

"You're pregnant." Holiday burst into tears, wrapping her arms around Tori. "We're going to be aunties," she cried.

I joined in the group hug, heart full and happy for my best friend.

25

I STARED AT THE BACK OF MY EYELIDS AND EXHALED. THE AWFUL noise of the MRI machine made relaxing difficult, but I was intent on staying still so I could get out of the enclosed space sooner rather than later.

After examining my knee, Noah had scheduled an MRI to make sure nothing had happened to my graft. He was afraid of a re-tear, which I didn't realize could even happen. Fortunately, I didn't have a fever or any signs of infection, because his first thought after seeing my swollen leg had been that my body was rejecting my graft.

I prayed not. I was already in pain from the healing my hamstring and knee were undergoing. If I had to have another surgery, that progress would be set back. I bit my lip as tears beat against my closed eyelids.

Lord, where are You? What are You doing in my life? I don't understand why rehab isn't going better. Don't You know I need to dance again?

Which, of course, He knew. But still, my life looked nothing like I'd pictured, and the need to express that had filled my soul.

Dancing had been my dream since my father had first

taken me to the ballet in Italy. Seeing the graceful way the ballerinas moved their bodies…how enraptured the crowd had been—specifically my father. All of it had put a deep yearning in my heart. When I told Babbo my dream of becoming a ballerina, he immediately contacted my mom to set up payment for lessons. I'd been dancing ever since.

Until now, waylaid by an injury I didn't see coming. It was one thing to injure myself during a performance and another having been attacked.

A tear spilled onto my cheek just as the exam bed jerked backward, slowly pulling me out of the machine. I scrambled to erase evidence of my sorrow and removed the ear plugs.

"You're all done, Ms. Ricci."

"Thank you." I took the offered hand and sat up, carefully swinging my leg around and coming to a stand. The stiffness was pretty uncomfortable, but at least my bruising from surgery had faded almost completely.

The technician handed me my crutches, and I went to the dressing room to put my own clothes back on. When I entered the waiting room, Noah sat hunched over his phone. He looked distracted, maybe even worried. Was something wrong?

"Hey."

He looked up and jumped to his feet. "All done?"

"Yep. Now to wait for the results."

"I'll see if we can get them expedited."

"Thank you. I appreciate that."

"Sure." He stared down at his cell as if willing it to chime with some important notification.

"Are you okay?"

"Um. My mom's been calling and texting. I had the phone on silent and didn't see the notifications until a few minutes ago. But when I tried to call back, she didn't answer."

I frowned. "Did she hurt herself?"

"No, no injuries." He swallowed. "Are you ready to go?"

Unease curled in my belly. "What's wrong with your mom, Noah?"

"She saw the pictures in the paper."

"Oh." I studied him. "You didn't tell her when they first released?"

"I did." He licked his lips. "After I talked with you."

"And she's just now seeing them?"

He nodded, a wariness in his gaze. As if he was waiting for me to put two and two together.

And how I wish that I hadn't. "She didn't know I'm Black," I whispered.

"Apparently not." He stepped forward. "Look, I told her we're going out. Told her I'm interested in you and that, even though you're a client, I want to date you. She was happy because she hates that I'm single." He ran a hand through his hair.

"But you didn't tell her I'm Black?"

"Come on, Octavia. I told her your name. She met you at the restaurant. Plus, who in the city doesn't know who you are?"

His mother apparently. But I clamped my lips closed, keeping my hurt and snark inside.

Noah took another step forward. "Octavia, please say something."

"Could you please drive me home?"

His lips turned downward, his puppy-dog eyes out in full force. "All right."

Silence stretched between us all the way back to my place and continued as he walked me to the front door. I turned, blocking his entry. "You should probably go talk to your mother."

"I plan to, but first, I need to know we're okay."

"Dr. Wright, we're just fine. I appreciate you making sure my leg—"

155

"Don't," he gritted through clenched teeth. "Don't do that."

But I had to. If I didn't, I'd break. Fall apart right in front of him and lose not only my composure but my dignity.

"Please let me know what the MRI says."

"Octavia."

I gulped. "Goodbye." I closed the door on his objections and turned the lock on his pleas.

As quickly and safely as possible, I maneuvered myself up a flight of stairs and headed for the living room. My mom sat on the settee with a book in hand.

"Mom, what are you doing here?"

"Holiday told me you hurt yourself." She arched an eyebrow to impressive heights. "Were you going to tell me?"

I nodded. "Waiting to find out the results from the MRI. I just returned from the hospital." I sank into a wingback chair, sighing as the strain on my leg eased.

"What do they think?"

"Right now, the doctor thinks I just overdid it on my last PT session." I'd been praying that was all ever since. "They're checking to make sure the graft has held and nothing else is wrong."

My mother nodded. "And when were you going to tell me you were dating someone?"

I sighed. "We've gone on one date. Well, two if you count dinner the other night. But we haven't labeled it. He knows I'm unsure of the whole situation."

"He seems nice. I'm a bit surprised you're dating your doctor though."

I rolled my eyes. "He recommended another PT specialist —the one who tried to kill me and reinjured my leg."

Her lips pursed. "Do you like him? Noah, I mean?"

Considering I went out on two dates with Noah, the question seemed pointless. But I knew my mom liked to ask a bunch of seemingly small questions until she threw a whopper out there. "Yes, Mom."

"And I imagine he likes you?"

I nodded.

"Then what's stopping you from labeling your relationship, Octavia? Or is he the one putting limits on you two?"

"No," I rasped. The memory of the hurt look on his face almost undid me.

She arched her eyebrow again, and I sighed. "I'm hesitant because of the race issue, Mom. And I just found out his mother may have a problem with me being Black."

"Why do you have a problem with an interracial relationship?"

I snorted. "Seeing you and Babbo ensured I had the perfect model for how *not* to be in a relationship."

"Octavia!" She gasped.

My eyes smarted. "I'm so sorry, Mom. I don't know what came over me." Despite the bitterness I felt, it was no reason to be disrespectful.

"I imagine you had some hurt you needed to let out," she said cautiously.

"Still, I shouldn't have said that."

"But it's true, isn't it?" Sadness covered her features, aging her in the process. "I never wanted our divorce to hurt you, sweetie. We thought separating was for the best. I had no idea it would affect your own relationships."

I opened my mouth to refute her claims. To reassure her ballet had been my one and only love and I'd never missed dating. But hadn't my words already hurt my mother enough? I didn't want her feeling worse than she already did. I'd never doubted her love for me.

She continued, oblivious to my inward struggles. "And you have to remember, you don't marry a person's family. Yes, you build relationships with their family, but it's not your primary focus or concern. Your spouse is. One hundred percent. Understand?"

"Yes, ma'am."

But even if my head understood all she said, my heart couldn't help but beat in pain at the thought of Noah's mother not liking me.

❦ 26 ❦

TWO DAYS LATER, MY CELL PHONE RANG, FLASHING NOAH'S number and the words *Dr. Right.* Noah had texted me plenty of times before now, but I'd ignored every single plea to talk in hope of shoring up my resolve. But that crumbled as the "Count on Me" ringtone continued playing.

"Hello?" As if I didn't know who was on the phone.

"Is this Octavia Ricci?"

Okay, maybe I didn't. My eyebrows shot up at the sound of a woman's voice. Noah's mother? I'd only been introduced to her that one time, but the voice sounded like hers. "Yes."

"This is Rina Wright, Noah's mom."

"Yes, ma'am." I honestly didn't know what else to say.

Her sigh was audible. "I'm sorry to bother you, but I feel the need to clear the air."

"O-kay." My mouth tripped over the words as my mind raced to possible scenarios and reasons for her call. Did she want to tell me her reaction had been a misunderstanding? That she didn't have a problem with me and to call Noah back and end his misery?

Or maybe I was the only one miserable in this scenario.

"I don't know how much my son has told you about my...reservations."

My shoulders sagged. "We haven't talked in a couple of days."

"Ah...I see. Ms. Ricci, since seeing that article, I've done my research. I can see you are a good girl. One who doesn't seek the spotlight off the stage."

Even I could sense the huge *but* she was about to vocalize along with a list of reasons why Noah and I wouldn't work out. Still, my upbringing wouldn't let me *not* participate in the conversation.

"I do try my best to live a quiet life." I winced, waiting for the proverbial shoe.

"I believe it, but you are one of two African American principal ballerinas. You're also the daughter of an Italian legend. I've often bought your father's wines. As much as you may like to ignore the spotlight, that light will still search for you."

I rubbed my forehead. "And that means?" I asked softly.

"I believe your relationship with my son is problematic. People will only see your stark differences. You understand this, don't you?"

I did. Hadn't that been one of my major objections from the get-go? But Noah had carved a niche in my heart that would leave a large hole with his absence. Could I actually step away permanently?

"And me never seeing him again would make your life so much easier, wouldn't it?" My eyes squeezed shut, horrified at my outburst. Just because I felt frustrated by her beliefs didn't mean I should regurgitate my feelings. "I'm sorry, Mrs. Wright. That was uncalled for."

"It's not. I called to have a candid conversation, and that will only work if you're honest."

I bit my lip. Someone wanting honest feelings from me felt a little suspect. She might as well have handed me a grenade with the pin missing. "I'm not sure what you want me to say, Mrs. Wright."

"I want to the truth. Do you really believe dating my son, risking him falling in love with you only for the outside world to come between you and leave hatred behind… Is it worth it? This relationship with my son?"

She acted like I had nefarious motives. I was a ballerina not a hitman. The only cutthroat behavior I exhibited was giving my all in a performance. "Are you asking me to not see him again?"

"I am. You must know, Ms. Ricci, deep in your heart. You must know you two will have constant opposition. What kind of life will you have? I've seen some of the hateful comments that followed after your news story."

Comments? What comments? "Where did you see them?"

She named a tabloid's website, and I typed my name and the headline in my internet search bar. As Mrs. Wright continued to monologue on the difficulties of interracial relationships, I reviewed the remarks at the end of the article.

My heart stopped.

My blood ran cold.

My pulse picked up speed as a roaring filled my ears. "Mrs. Wright, I have to go."

I didn't wait for an objection or an acceptance, simply ended the call as my eyes scanned comment after comment of hate. Some of the remarks were tame, not understanding what the problem was since I wasn't really Black but mixed. Didn't surprise me. But the others were so awful my stomach lurched and the contents swirled.

Never55: He's going to dilute our gene pool.

Maisy123: She's a sellout.

Purenation1: No, I think he is.

Blackpride29: Wow, back in the day, our ancestors were raped, now she's just giving it away for free?

My mouth turned acrid, and I raced to the bathroom,

barely crossing the threshold in time to lose my lunch. Heave after heave pummeled my stomach as my mind replayed the mocking tone of the critics. Filled my head and heart with their hatred.

Tears streamed down my face. I couldn't do this. I couldn't be in a relationship with Noah. My life would be easier if I just went it alone. Kept to myself like I'd been doing all my adult life. I didn't need a man, certainly not one that would have the trolls of society making my life miserable. Hadn't I already been targeted enough?

After all, living a solo life had worked for my mother for decades, why not me? Nowhere in the Bible was marriage commanded and listed as a Christian requirement. Paul did say some were called to a single life and could even better serve God that way. Maybe that was my lot.

My hope of the *someday* dream of being a wife and mother disintegrated with each drop of my tears. I'd been so foolish to believe that my feelings, my wants, my desires could survive the onslaught of other people's beliefs.

I closed my eyes, leaning against the bathroom cabinets.

Lord, please restore my dream of dancing if I cannot have my someday *dream. I need something to hold onto. Something to motivate me and give me hope.*

"Let us hold fast the confession of our hope without wavering, for He who promised is faithful."

The verse from Hebrews echoed in my thoughts. What was the Spirit trying to tell me? That I would dance again? Or to keep hold of my *someday* dream? *Or* was He leading to a simpler way of thinking that held a far-reaching impact for my life. Spiritual and mental?

"Let us hold fast the confession of our hope without wavering, for He who promised is faithful."

I had long since confessed my need for Jesus, who was my hope. He promised to be faithful to me, and that faith would see me in Heaven. That was simply Christianity 101 and what all new believers were taught. But when had I let the simplicity of that knowledge turn into something I'd taken for granted? I'd moved that knowledge from my *learned and understood* box to *yeah, yeah, I get it.*

Shame heated my cheeks and tears coursed faster down my face.

I'm so sorry that I've taken You for granted. That confessing my need for You made me forget how I will always need You. Nothing else. Just You. Only You to fill up every crevice in my life. To be my answer to every problem. Whether I dance again. Whether I will see my dreams come to fruition one day. But even if I don't, I will always have my first love: You.

I sniffed as peace filled my heart. God forgave me. I could feel that truth as sure as I could feel the ache in my knee. Knew He would always forgive me when I came to Him in true repentance. And the icing on top of the cake? He would never leave me the same way I came.

I wasn't sure what would happen going forward, but finally, for the first time in so long, I felt His presence once more. The loneliness had lifted as I sat there knowing God was here. I wasn't alone.

Never had been, truly. I'd just misaligned my focus for a moment.

I see clearly now, Lord. I'm looking to You. Reaching for Your love in a sea of hate. Please help me not let animosity or bitterness find fertile ground in my heart. May I only water my soul with the seeds of Your love. Amen.

❧ 27 ❧

MY ORTHOPEDIC SURGEON FINALLY CALLED WITH THE NEWS. MY graft had been torn. I was now a candidate for revision ACL reconstruction surgery.

I couldn't even cry, the news so stunned me. Only the doctor's repeated question penetrated the haze of my brain fog.

"Do you want to have the second surgery? I know how important getting back to dancing is for you."

"Then you think this will give me that chance?" I was barely holding on to the dream of dancing again, let alone at principal level.

"Yes. But I must warn you, this will lengthen your recovery time. You can't rush yourself."

"*I* didn't. *That* doctor did." Anger simmered as reality sank in.

"I understand," he responded cautiously. "Would you like me to request Dr. Wright to reach out to you again? I believe he was the one who took you to the MRI appointment."

A lump formed in my throat. How I wanted to curl up in Noah's arms and sob my guts out. Let him sing to me about how he would always be there. But the cautionary words of his mother and the vitriol of the social media trolls slammed a door on that desire.

"No. Please find me another concierge physical therapist. I already have an exam table in my home." I curled an arm around my stomach, imagining what Noah would say when he found out. *If* he found out.

"Will do. I will have the nurse contact you with your options."

"Thank you."

"Sure thing. Please hold and I'll transfer you to my scheduler. Okay?"

I nodded, then croaked out my verbal agreement.

Another surgery. Longer recovery. No Noah.

I slid my forehead into my hand as the weight of the news pushed down on me. How would I get through this? Maybe I needed to sit and pray for a new dream. One that didn't involve dancing. One that didn't involve the blushes and moon eyes my roommates—well, one former roomie—were experiencing. I always did have to do life differently.

The scheduler penciled me in for two weeks to the day due to a cancellation they'd received. The assistant warned I would have waited another month if it hadn't been for the opening, prolonging my healing even further. I thanked him then texted my mom.

O: I REINJURED MY ACL AND HAVE TO HAVE ANOTHER SURGERY IN TWO WEEKS. I DON'T FEEL LIKE TALKING ABOUT IT RIGHT NOW. WILL YOU BE THERE?

M: OF COURSE.

I pulled up the group text with Holiday and Tori, copying and pasting the same message I'd sent to my mom.

H: OH, SWEETIE! THAT'S AWFUL.

OF COURSE I'LL BE THERE.

T: I WILL BE THERE TOO. IS THERE ANYTHING I CAN DO?

DO YOU NEED ICE CREAM?

Movie night?

H: Spa day?

I sighed, staring at the message through suspiciously dry eyes. As much as I wanted their company, I needed to let them live their lives. Tori was now expecting a baby. Holiday would be married in the summer but had already begun creating a life with her and Emmett. Maybe now was the time to find a new way to honor God and throw myself into a singles ministry.

O: That's not necessary. I'm just going to let the news soak in.

T: Are you sure? I can be there soon.

H: Yeah, you never turn down a spa day.

O: I really don't want to go down the stairs.

T: Good point

H: Good point

I laughed. Even in text they often parroted one another. I exited out of the app and lay on my back. Later, I'd email the company and tell them the news. I didn't have the energy to do so now.

An hour later, a rap sounded at the door. "Come in."

"Hey, girl." Holiday smiled softly at me.

"Hey." I rubbed the sleep from my eyes. "What's up?"

"Since you didn't want to go to the spa, I brought the spa to you."

"What?" I straightened.

Holiday gestured down my hall toward the studio. "Called in a favor, and I've got a masseuse, stylist, and makeup artist here for girl time."

"Holiday…" I struggled to rise, then wrapped an arm around her waist. "Thank you."

"Anytime. No matter what happens, we'll be friends forever. Which means if you need me, I'm there."

I sniffed. "You can't guarantee that. One day your family will come before me."

She brushed my hair back from my face. "You *are* my family."

Love filled my heart. *Thank You Lord for wonderful friends.*

We walked to my studio, and I smiled at the sight. A massage table had been set up in one corner, a pedicure chair in another, and a stylist section had been erected in the center of the room. They'd even brought rubber mats to protect my floor from their equipment.

"This is amazing."

"Agreed. Tori's downstairs grabbing snacks. She'll be up in a second."

I nodded.

"What do you want to do first? Massage? Pedicure? I figure makeup will be last."

"Who did you get for makeup?" I frowned, eyeing the ladies, trying to match up their stations with the services Holiday said she'd requested.

"Sasha." She beamed. "She's started a makeup vlog. Tori promised her an exclusive look at her natural face and then all glammed up, but only if Sasha uses the products Tori has a contract with. She'll make you and me up for free. We won't even have to worry about being caught on video. That's all Tori."

"Sasha's such a sweetheart." I looked around the room and stopped on the stylist. My hand came up, fingering my hair. "Haircut," I whispered.

"What?" Holiday's eyes grew wide and she licked her lips nervously. "Are you sure that's not a little cliché?"

"No one pointed out your coping mechanisms when your dad married stepmother number five."

Her lips pursed. "Fine." She extended a hand toward the chair. "Knock yourself out."

"Who's knocking who out?" Tori asked as she waltzed in with two trays of food. Sasha trailed her, holding a tray of drinks.

I frowned as I spied my father's pinot noir. "No wine for me, please."

If I weren't Donovan Ricci's daughter, would the social media backlash have been so disastrous when pictures of Noah and me were leaked?

Tori nodded and opened a can of flavored sparkling water.

"Tavia wants her hair cut," Holiday chimed.

"Makes sense. In what style?" Tori asked.

Holiday's mouth dropped open. "You're not going to tell her it's a bad idea?"

"No one stopped you from jumping off the ledge that was an insane dye job after your father married stepmother number...what?" She looked at me. "Six?"

"Pretty sure it was five." My lips twitched.

"And you call yourselves my best friends." Holiday pouted.

I chuckled, relieved I could still find something to laugh about. But really, visualizing Holiday with that bright green hair always made me chuckle. She couldn't dye her hair back quick enough.

I made my way over to the stylist.

"Hi, Ms. Ricci." She smiled and held out a hand. "I'm Serenity. Do you just want a wash and style?"

"I'd like a cut, actually."

"Okay. Any particular length in mind?"

I shook my head. Who knew if I'd get back to my pointe shoes? I didn't need to worry about putting my hair in a bun. "Whatever you think will look best."

"Yes!" She rubbed her hands together with glee. "You're in good hands. Have a seat."

She washed my hair, which felt marvelous. It was like a massage for my head—one that instantly made me sleepy. Then she cut my hair, blow dried it straight, and cut it some more, all the while keeping a running dialogue about the city and how different New York was from her hometown in Texas. She didn't really have an accent—at least not a deep south one—though I did hear a slight inflection in her voice.

I wanted to peek at the mirror, but she kept my back to my reflection during the entire process. By the time she was done, I'd made up my mind to head for the masseuse next.

"You ready?"

"Yes." I straightened my shoulders and braced myself as Serenity turned the chair around to face the mirror.

I gasped. My hair stopped at my chin in a blunt bob. She'd added light brown streaks to my darker ones, brightening my face. It would take some getting used to, but I liked it. A new me. A new outside to match the commitment I'd given God on the inside. I would embrace singlehood with joy, even if it broke everything else within me.

❧ 28 ❧

I INHALED THE CRISP AIR, LETTING MY LUNGS OPEN. PROOF OF life and a reminder of God's blessing this morning. If breathing wasn't enough to break through my thoughts, the beautiful sunrise confirming God's handiwork would. The beauty of the blues and oranges hitting the skyline took my breath away. It reminded me of one of my favorite verses from Psalm 145: *"I will meditate on the glorious splendor of Your majesty, And on Your wondrous works."*

God had left His fingerprints on the world for us to enjoy. A visual compass to point to Him and show us who He is. The great Creator. A Master artist.

I cleared my mind of all that wasn't Him, knowing my racing thoughts on life would pick up sooner than I'd like. For now, it was just me and the Lord as I sat there on the rooftop. Believing that I wasn't alone. Something I had so desperately needed to know.

God had never left me. I'd turned my eyes away from Him, taken my focus off Him, and stopped seeking Him first. But now I was back on track. I'd read my Bible this morning. Taken notes on how I felt. Talked to Him about what I'd learned. It had been gloriously normal and much yet more at the same time.

Thank You for showing me You're still with me. For forgiving me for taking my eyes off You.

I inhaled gratitude and exhaled through the peace cloaking me like the violins that swirled in the ballet orchestra of my mind. I rose slowly and turned to head downstairs. The doctor had said I could take the stairs as long as I used my crutches to not put weight on my injured leg. I needed to make my way to the kitchen for nourishment and a plan for the day.

The room was empty, and I smiled. There was nothing like a quiet kitchen before noise broke through the home and signaled the start of the day. I'd always felt these peaceful moments were a way to extend my time with the Lord. I'd make an espresso as I planned out my meals and agenda for the day while my thoughts stayed connected to Him.

Right now, I needed a ministry. If dancing wouldn't be on my radar for the foreseeable future, then something had to take its place. I couldn't stand being idle.

Lord, where do you want me? How can I help?

I pulled out a notepad that I kept in one of the drawers for moments like this and flipped to a clean page. After writing *Ideas* at the top, I jotted a couple down.

1. Ask church if they need help in any areas
2. Ask ballet studios if they need assistance

I paused, rereading that last line. I couldn't dance right now, but I had years of experience that would be useful to those rising through the ranks. Hadn't Noah reminded me about mentoring others? I'd offered words of encouragement or advice when I was with the Company, but it wasn't something I'd consciously done. Well, maybe in a way it was. I'd never wanted to have that prima donna persona—too many doors had closed in my face because of those types—so I had gone out of my way to help others, offer tips.

If one dancer looked bad, we all did. If one shone, we all shone. Maybe that could be my new way to help. What was the Bible always admonishing? Think of others, *esteem* others better than ourselves? This was a way I could do that. I wrote names of those who may need help or be able to steer me in the right direction under the second idea.

"You look extra perky this morning," Holiday groused from the doorway.

I arched an eyebrow. "Should I make you a cup of coffee?"

"Already ordered some and an everything bagel."

I wrinkled my nose.

"Don't worry, I ordered some gross quinoa meal. Apparently, the fruit in it makes it fit for breakfast." She made a gagging motion with her finger.

"I love you." I giggled.

"Love you too, Tavia." She shuffled over to me and gave me a hug, then looked down at my list. "What's this?"

"I need a new purpose. I was brainstorming."

"I see you like the second idea."

I nodded.

"You'd be good at that. What if you open your own studio?"

My eyes bugged out. "What?" I squeaked.

"You could certainly afford to. And if you targeted the minorities and lower income communities, those who dream but see no way of obtaining that...think of the good you could do."

"Hol, that's an amazing idea." I paused, mulling over her words. Examining the feelings that were bubbling in my chest. This had weight. Had meaning. "I'll pray about this."

"And I'll pray He gives you clarity." She pointed to the other side of the island. "I forgot. You have a letter. Came yesterday." She handed it to me.

I stared at the white envelope, stilling as *Noah Wright* jumped out at me.

"I couldn't help but notice the good doctor's name."

"I'm sure you couldn't," I murmured.

Holiday laughed. "I'll go get dressed. That way you can read it in peace."

I barely nodded as the sound of her slippered feet faded. I grabbed the letter opener out of the drawer to my right and sliced the envelope open. Two pages had been folded in thirds. I opened it, smoothing out the indents as I rested it on the countertop.

Dear Octavia,

I've thought of countless ways to start this letter. In fact, the trashcan next to me might have a few earlier drafts that were too awful to mail out. And, honestly, I'm not even sure this one fully encompasses what I want to say.

I hope you'll read this and not throw it away. I figured a letter might have more impact than the texts you've blocked and the emails you've deleted, though I know you received them.

I winced at his brutal honesty, but still felt right in my decision. If I'd opened his emails, if I hadn't blocked him, my resolve would have crumpled in a heartbeat.

I want to start with the most glaring issue: my mother. She confessed about her phone call and how you ended the call shortly after it began. And to have a full picture, I read the comments from that article and put two and two together. But you have to realize that it's an addition problem, not subtraction. You removing yourself from my life doesn't make anything better. It makes it worse. After all, the Bible tells us two are better than one.

If our Heavenly Father didn't want His children to be alone, why won't you give me a chance? Why would you dump me before I could ever offer for us to go steady? (Is that too cheesy? Too light-hearted for the moment? I apologize and will get back on topic).

My lips twitched.

We can't live to please men. God wants us to serve Him. Not people. Not their beliefs, expectations, etc. Especially when their opinions have no basis in His word. Those comments in the article weren't God-honoring. If this had been the Old Testament, they'd all be stricken down by leprosy. Man created racial problems, not God. He sees no partiality with men, so why would He see it in relationships?

I'm writing to ask that you give us a chance. To see if we fit. To see if we could have a forever happiness. If you're going to dump me, do it because our personal differences are too big to overcome, not because my skin is lighter than yours.

Please know I'm praying for you. Every day. I'm praying for your healing. I'm praying for your peace of mind. I'm praying you feel God's presence saturate you to your core.

Until next time,

Noah

❧ 29 ❧

I inhaled the notes of frigid air and sweat that made up the aroma of the ballet studio. Giselle had asked me to stop by so we could talk about ways I could assist her. She was the only person who'd seemed willing to help me. The others were all too busy or in crises of their own.

My nerve endings twitched as I waited in the seating area with the parents. Almost all had some sort of electronic device in their hands. One even had a laptop open, her fingers clicking across the keys. Obviously, I should have brought a book or something to occupy my time.

I thought of Noah's letter—I'd read it four more times already—on my nightstand. I'd put the envelope in my drawer but had left the pages under my ballerina figurine. As if reading his words just one more time would connect me to him.

I wasn't sure what rereading would accomplish. So far, only intense yearning for his presence. For the easy conversation and laughter that had flowed between us before the news article. He was right, I hadn't dumped him for any other reason than what other people thought of us together. But other people's opinions—especially vitriolic ones—shouldn't have power over my life. Shouldn't be deal breakers.

I paused. Did I have any of those? What was a good reason for dumping someone?

Disagreeing on kids?

Finances?

The desire to make another list pricked at me, and I pulled out my cell to open a note app. I already knew I wanted kids. The question was how many, was I flexible, and what happened if I couldn't have them? I wrote these questions down only to have others follow.

Joint account or separate?

Prenup or not?

My father would probably insist on a prenup, considering I would inherit a portion of the winery upon his passing.

Specific Christian denomination or flexible as long as doctrinally sound?

Public school or private?

As much as I appreciated my father paying for my education, going to private school had been hard. Sure, I'd had my friendship with Tori and Holiday, but I didn't get to see my mom unless it was the weekend and she drove up from the city to our school in Connecticut.

As I mulled over the questions, I wrote my answers as they came to me.

At least two kids but willing to go up to four. If we cannot have any for whatever reason, willing to discuss alternatives including no kids.

Joint. I don't want to hide money or worry about my spouse not trusting me.

Maybe some clause that will protect the other Ricci heirs but won't deny my kids a legacy.

Flexible as long as we agree the church is the best for our family.

No boarding schools. Can discuss pros and cons of public and private school.

I bit my lip, unblocked Noah's settings in my cell, then typed in a new message.

O: Do you want kids?

I stared at the screen, waiting to see if he would respond immediately or not.

N: She lives.

I chuckled.

O: Sorry. How are you?

N: I'm good, and yes, I want kids.

O: How many?

N: At least two.

O: What if you can't have any?

N: Why not?

N: You mean an infertility struggle?

O: Yes.

I blew out a breath as I waited for his three dots to stop undulating. What was taking him so long?

N: I don't know because I can't imagine the heartache that comes with that and how I would respond. Would I want to seek infertility treatments? Adopt? Foster? I just don't know. It's definitely something I would take step by step with my wife.

N: Why do you ask?

O: I'm comparing our personal differences.

N: Is this the part where I act all cool instead of doing a fist pump?

I laughed at the Breakfast Club GIF he sent me of John Bender throwing a fist in the air.

O: Looks like you lost your cool points already.

N: Sorry, I love GIFs.

O: Me too. It's my third fluent language.

N: English and Italian being the first two?

O: Oops, fourth

N: What's the third?

O: Ballet

N: Duh

N: Any other questions you want to ask me?

O: I have a whole list but also I have an appointment and need to go right now.

N: Then I can text you later?

I drew in a ragged breath. If I wanted to ask him questions, he should be allowed the same courtesy. But I was still scared.

O: For personal differences purposes only

N: Got it.

I put my phone in my purse as moms filed out of the studio with their exhausted children. I scanned the area looking for Giselle. Would she change first? Had she forgotten she'd asked me to show up? Before I could worry further, she came out of the studio and into the waiting area.

I stood, hating the soreness in my armpits. I was so very tired of crutches.

"Octavia." She kissed my left cheek then my right. "It's great to see you. I was sad to hear of your injury."

"You and me both."

"Let's talk in my office."

I followed Giselle, scanning the studio as we passed through to her office. Her mirrors didn't have a speck of dust on them and made the room seem brighter and bigger than it really was.

As we entered her office, Giselle pointed to the chair next to her desk. I sank into the seat as she settled behind her desk.

"How are you recovering? Will you be able to dance professionally again?"

"Honestly, I don't know. I'll be having another surgery soon."

"Oh, Octavia. That's awful."

I nodded, accepting her sympathy, knowing full well how much she understood. Giselle had broken her leg in a freak accident, falling off the stage during a performance. She never danced professionally again.

I cleared my throat. "The surgery will push my recovery back another six months."

"And you're trying to figure out what to do in the meantime?"

"Yes."

She smiled, her eyes assessing me. I resisted the urge to fidget under her gaze. Her blonde hair had been pulled back in an elegant bun. Lines framed her mouth as her lips pursed with thought.

"Do you just want to mentor or take a more active role?"

Good question. I spread my hands out. "I'm flexible. My doctor thinks I'll be allowed activity in a couple of months. If you have girls ready for recitals around that time, I can come in and assist. Or be a backup to teach a class if you need one." I bit my lip. "That is, if I don't have to do the moves."

"Octavia," she said with a slow smile, "I think you are an answer to my prayer."

"You do?" I struggled to keep the shock out of my voice. Not what I'd thought she would say.

She smiled, her ruby-red lips widening. "Yes. I'm ready to retire. But this place, it's my heart, and I cannot just leave it unattended."

My mouth dropped. Was she saying—

"Yes." She nodded. "I need to leave this place in good hands."

"How do you know I'm that person?"

She tapped a finger over her heart. "I feel it. But you may not be where I'm at in the decision process. That's okay. Go home. Pray about it. Until then, I can certainly add you to help teach some classes once the doctor clears you for long periods of standing. We can ease you in then, and hopefully, soon you can dance. Experience is often the best indicator of whether you will be the right fit to run a business."

"Thank you so much, Giselle." I had a plan. Well, a fluid one.

"My pleasure."

We air kissed, then I left, thinking the whole way. Thankfully, Mac had waited for me and was ready to take me back home, where I could pray and decide if owning a studio was really an option. Hadn't Holiday just suggested it? And Giselle was ready to retire? Was that a sign from God that this was my new dream? My new path?

I just didn't know.

❧ 30 ❧

I MOANED AS AN INTENSE STAB OF PAIN THREATENED TO ENGULF me. I tried to swallow, but my mouth felt drier than after a performance.

"Ms. Ricci? Are you in pain?"

I tried to say yes. Tried to lift a hand as an affirmative, but only a low moan fell between my lips. Had I felt this bad after my first surgery?

A warm hand covered mine. "Ms. Ricci, squeeze my hand if you're in a lot of pain."

I squeezed.

"I'm going to get you some more meds. Hang in there, hon."

I tried to lift my head, but it felt too heavy. I hoped the nurse knew how thankful I was for her assistance. How many medical staff helped a patient through surgery and never received thanks? Not for lack of appreciation, but just because we were unconscious or hazed with pain?

"Ms. Ricci, I'm back. I'm putting some pain meds in your IV right now."

I licked my lips. "Thank you," I croaked.

"You're very welcome. Besides the pain, are you having any other discomfort?"

I shook my head.

"Okay. Just rest. Let the medicine do its job."

I closed my eyes and soon drifted back to sleep. When I woke again, I lay in a private room. My eyes scanned the area. I vaguely remembered talking to Holiday in the recovery room. Was she still here? I sighed with relief as I spotted Holiday and Tori by the window. Their voices were low, heads bent close together.

"Hey." I cleared my throat, trying to speak around the dryness.

"You're awake." Holiday smiled and came to stand by the bed. "Do you need some water?"

I nodded and she handed me a mug, the straw pointed toward my mouth. I drank, sighing as it quenched the parched places in my mouth. I took a few more sips then passed it back. "I hurt."

Tori came to stand opposite Holiday.

"I bet." Holiday ran a hand over my hair. "But the doctor said the surgery went well and the tear wasn't as bad as he thought, so he didn't have to take a lot of tissue to graft a new one."

"It feels worse than last time."

"He said it would," Tori stated. "Because you were still healing from the last one."

"Oh." I closed my eyes, breathing through the pain.

"Are you still tired?" Holiday asked softly.

"No. Just weary."

"Are you up for visitors?" Tori asked.

"You two are already here. Or do you mean my mom?" She'd been here, waiting with me before surgery started. Where had she gone?

"She went to grab some lunch, but she'll be back. I was talking about the good doctor though."

My eyes flew open, and Holiday winked. "Noah's here?"

She and Tori both nodded.

I bit my lip. "I look a mess, don't I?"

Tori laughed. "You look just fine. Do you want me to grab him?"

"Okay."

I looked at Holiday as Tori left the room. "What am I supposed to say to him?"

"Whatever needs to be said." She squeezed my hand. "You've got this. I'll see you later, all right?"

I nodded and she left me alone to fret while I waited for Noah to stop in.

A knock sounded. "Come in."

Noah walked in, looking slightly hesitant. My pulse raced as I took him in. It felt like forever since I'd seen him. And even though we'd been texting every single day and he'd sent another letter, seeing him in person was completely different.

"How are you feeling?" He ran a hand through his brown hair.

"Like I've been cut open and sewn back together again."

He laughed. "Yeah, imagine that." He made his way next to me, eyeing me with every step that brought us closer. He finally stopped, resting his hand on the bed rail. "I like your hair cut."

I blinked at the unexpected pronouncement. "Thanks." I ran a hand down my shortened locks. "I didn't expect to see you."

His eyebrows rose expectantly. "Where else would I be?"

"With your family? Friends? Clients?"

"I thought we were at least friends, if nothing else."

I bit my lip. "We are."

"Then I'm right where I need to be."

My heart warmed, but then I thought of his mother. "What would your mom say?"

His green eyes roamed my face, an intense gleam darkening the pupils. "It doesn't matter. What matters is what I said to her."

My brows rose, waiting for his explanation.

"I told her that this thing between us is worth exploring, worth seeing if it could be something more, and that meant I would be here when you woke up."

My lips twitched. "I didn't think to ask you to come."

"Why not?"

I shrugged a shoulder. Making a decision to date Noah wasn't something I wanted to do lightly, and if I wasn't ready to say yes to that, what right did I have to ask him to come to my surgery? Instead of saying all of that, I merely met his gaze.

"Haven't you figured out by now that if you need me, I'll be there?"

My heart skipped. "Maybe I'm starting to get a clue."

"Well, clearly, you need glasses to see my breadcrumbs."

I grinned. "Are you calling me blind?"

"Obviously."

I laughed outright then groaned.

Noah winced. "Maybe take it easy there."

"You made me laugh."

"I won't do it again."

"Likely story."

His lip quirked into that half smile that made my heart want to dive for my toes. My cell blared, the ringtone breaking through our moment. I looked at the stand next to me, reaching for the annoying device. It was my dad. Huh.

"Buongiorno, Babbo."

"Mi piccolina. You are well?"

"I hurt, Babbo."

"*Sono così dispiaciuto.*"

His *I'm so sorry* soothed me. "It's okay."

"It is not. I was thinking. My daughter is having another surgery, and I have not been there for her."

My mouth parted.

"So I say to myself, Donovan, you need to see your daughter."

My breath hitched. "You're coming to New York?" I couldn't remember the last time he'd visited.

"I am already here. Your mother thought I should call before stopping by your room."

"You didn't have to. You're my father. You can visit me any time."

"Good. I must meet this young man. Noah, is it?"

My eyes flew to Noah. I didn't know if he could hear my father, but he held a *what is it?* expression on his face.

"Yes."

"Bene. I will see you soon."

I put the phone down. "My father wants to meet you."

"Seems fair since you've met some of my family."

"Are we at the meeting the family stage?"

"I think we're winging it."

"Are you nervous?"

"Not in the least." He smiled.

Someone knocked on my door before pushing it open. My father walked in. He wore a long-sleeve sweater over a collared shirt, his slacks creased to perfection. His style of casual.

"Piccolina." He threw his hands in the air then bent to kiss me on the forehead. "You look tired."

"*Un po.*" I held my thumb and pointer finger slightly apart. My eyes darted to Noah then back to my father. "Babbo, this is Dr. Noah Wright, my friend." Would he hate that title? A quick glance showed an easy smile on Noah's face. "Noah, this is my father, Donovan Ricci."

"Nice to meet you, sir." Noah extended his hand over the bed, and my father shook it.

"You are a physical therapist, yes?"

"I am, but I'm here as a friend, not a medical

professional."

"Yes." My father rubbed his hairless chin. He'd never been one for facial hair, preferring a clean-cut look. "I saw you in the papers."

I winced.

"Um, yes. Unfortunately, a lot of people have."

"Why unfortunate?" My father crossed his arms.

What was he doing? Was he really trying to interrogate Noah? My eyes kept darting back and forth to keep up with the conversation.

"It was a private moment that should have stayed that way."

"Then perhaps you should not kiss in public."

Kill me now. I tugged on my blanket, hoping to raise it over my head without them noticing. Obviously, I didn't need to be party to this discussion.

"I do apologize for that, sir. I was…overcome."

My face couldn't warm any more. If the pain from surgery didn't kill me, embarrassment would.

"Piccolina, what are you doing?" My father tugged my blanket down.

"Hiding."

He shook his head. "We are simply talking."

"As if I'm not here."

My father looked at me in surprise.

I rarely talked to him like this, so I shouldn't have been shocked he was shocked. "Sorry, Babbo."

"Perhaps I will take your friend for some coffee. Then you can get some rest."

I stared at Noah.

"I'll be fine." He winked.

I nodded, too stunned to say anything else.

"Bene. It is done. We will be back. Get some rest." My father bent down and kissed my cheek. "Ti amo."

"Love you too, Babbo."

31

My parents were driving me insane!

If I had to hear them bicker one more time, I would kick them out. Not that my father was staying at my place. He'd checked himself into a hotel the day he arrived in the city, but he spent the majority of his time with me—and my mother.

I winced as the sound of their angry whispers filtered through the living room. My father had carried me down the stairs to enjoy breakfast and a movie. Then my mother had decided that she would watch TV with us as well. Next thing I knew, they were arguing over who dunnit in the murder-mystery I'd picked out.

They had finally retreated to the kitchen under the guise of retrieving movie snacks. In reality, they wanted to continue their "discussion."

"That woman!" My father ran a hand through his locks, every line on his face turning south with irritation as he stomped into the living room.

"I don't know why you even start."

"She is maddening. I'm going to have to get my blood pressure checked when I go back home."

I bit back a laugh. "Maybe a glass of wine will soothe you."

"It is too early." He checked his wristwatch and shook his head, sinking into the wingback chair nearest the sofa. "Piccolina, I may return home tomorrow."

I sat up. "So soon?"

"Your stepmother, she wants me back home. And the business…" He shrugged. "Well, I must run it."

"I understand." I offered a smile to show I didn't hold any hard feelings. Because for the first time, I truly didn't. He'd come to spend time with me. Our relationship felt like it was in a better place. "Thank you for staying as long as you have."

"But of course. You are part of my heart. I needed to make sure you were okay."

I stared at the empty doorway behind him, then bit my lip as my gaze assessed him. "Babbo, can I ask you a question?"

"Sure." He shifted forward. "What is it?"

Tears blurred my vision. I needed to ask him. Hated to even hear the answer, but I could no longer bury my head in the sand. "Why did you and mom divorce?"

He hooked his thumb over his shoulder and snorted. "You have to ask? We could not stop fighting. Always with the fighting."

"And that was it? Just fighting?" *Not race, nationality, or me?*

"That question is not so simple." He stretched his legs before me. "That was it and it was not. The fighting"—he waved a hand in the air—"nonstop. What had been a passionate love turned into a volatile marriage. We could not start a conversation without turning it into an argument. I wanted you to have a pacifier, your mom did not. I wanted cloth diapers, she wanted disposable ones. If we could pick opposite sides, we did. Not to be contrary but because we were just so very different."

"Then how did you even fall in love?"

He grinned. "Your mother is beautiful. And I am a sucker for a beautiful woman."

I laughed even as my cheeks heated with embarrassment.

He reached over and squeezed my hand. "It was never about you. The reason we divorced. The only reason we managed to be together as long as we were was because we did not want to destroy your life. My family was very upset with me when I divorced your mother. I was the first one in our family to do so. They were ashamed." He turned, staring ahead unseeingly.

My eyes widened. "Is that why they don't like me?"

"Bah. You cannot listen to my mother. She is old. Old people stick to the ways they know, afraid to stretch and grow. And however she feels, you are her grandchild. That, she will never deny."

But he didn't deny Grandmama had a problem with me. It hurt, but it wasn't a surprise. Just one of the reasons I often avoided her.

"But everyone else loves you, piccolina."

"I don't know. I've heard some remarks here and there."

"Ah, yes. I took those people aside." His brow furrowed. "They did not still say mean things to you, did they?"

"No, *Babbo*. I just never really felt a part of the family."

He sighed. "I am sorry, piccolina. As much as I tried not to hurt you, I *have* hurt you. But I do not regret marrying your mother. I would not have you if I hadn't."

"Grazie, Babbo."

He chucked my chin. "Now, let's talk about this Noah."

"No. Let's not." I groaned, squeezing my eyes shut.

"I like him."

"You do?" I pried an eye open to study my father.

"I do." He nodded. "He is a quiet man. A steady man. And he seems to care for you very much."

"Our one date caused a ruckus in the social media world."

"Eh, people believe what they believe."

189

"People believe what?" my mom asked as she sauntered into the room with bowls of popcorn.

"Our daughter has been hearing dissent regarding her relationship with the doctor."

My mom cocked a hand on her hip. "You're not still letting that get to you, are you?" At my silence, she forged ahead, taking a seat on the couch with me. "You ignore them. They're not the ones living your life."

I glanced from my mom to my father, then down to my hands. "Don't you think interracial relationships are hard?" My soft voice echoed in the quiet.

Silence beat in the room as thoughtful expressions filled my parents' faces.

"For me," my father began, "it was not our race that made our marriage hard. It was our differences and lack of compromise. I did not want to compromise and neither did your mother."

"True," my mom agreed.

"Paulina and I are more alike, but we also work hard to reach compromises for those hard-to-make choices. It was a promise I made—not to be so stubborn."

My mom snickered, but she composed herself when my father fell silent. "I've never worried about dating someone outside my race," my mom added. "If I like the man and he's interested, I'll go out on a date." She looked at me. "But I'm not in the limelight like you are either." A wistful smile filled her face. "My friends all thought your father was good looking. Once we married, their worry was about him being from Italy and wanting to go back there."

"Ah, yes. I am attached to my vineyards."

"And I'm attached to America." My mother shrugged. "Like your father said. We didn't want to compromise, and I gave him an ultimatum."

"What?" My head swiveled between them.

"You did not tell her?" My father asked, eyebrows shooting high.

My mom shook her head then looked me in the eyes. "Your father wanted to raise you in Italy for the first year. After six months, I couldn't take it. I was going crazy and wanted to be back in New York. I finally told him that I couldn't live there any longer and needed to go back." She glanced at him then back at me.

"He suggested I take a vacation and spend some time with my old friends. I told him if I did, I wouldn't come back. He insisted a vacation would be good for me, and that he would happily watch over you so I could decompress." My mom looked away and her voice dropped to a whisper. "I told him I wasn't leaving you. You were coming with me."

"I told her she could not just take you away. You were my daughter," my father continued in a stronger voice.

"But I wouldn't listen." My mom wiped at her face. "I told him if he didn't let us leave, I would make sure he never saw you again and would sue him for his winery shares."

My mouth dropped. How had I never heard this story? They'd always told me they couldn't get along, but I'd never imagined this. I thought their differences stemmed from their race.

"If he would agree to let us go," my mother's voice whispered, "I would ensure he could see you every summer and would not ask for alimony or anything else."

"Mom…"

"I know." Her voice cracked as tears spilled down her cheeks. "I don't know if I was suffering from postpartum depression or just young and foolish. I really left your father with no choice." She looked at him. "I'm sorry, Donovan."

"I forgave you a long time ago, Angela."

"Thank you."

"Then race *wasn't* an issue for you two?" How could that

not be? Didn't they hear the snide comments people threw their way?

"No. That's not to say we didn't run into people who exercised their mouths a little too much for our liking. But we weren't going to let it stop us." My mom cupped my face. "And if you really like Noah, then don't let it stop you either."

I sighed, my mind reeling from all the information they'd shared. My parents had certainly given me a lot to think about.

32

THE BLISTERING AIR GREETED ME AS I WALKED INTO GISELLE'S studio. Light poured into the room, and I sighed with pure pleasure at the barre. How I wished I could do my own warm-up, but I was a long way from that. For now, I would have to wait. Today, I would be shadowing Giselle as she taught a class and showed me what she expected from her students *and* her teachers.

Strands of Tchaikovsky's *Swan Lake* filtered through the studio speakers as girls filed in and took their places in front of the barre. I lowered myself into the seat in the back that I assumed had been placed there for me to watch the class. Six girls had walked in, which meant either Giselle kept her classes really small or some of the girls had yet to arrive.

I glanced at the time on my cell. Ten minutes until class started.

The studio door opened, and another teen hustled toward the barre. Her gaze scanned the room and landed on me. She froze, and her mouth dropped open. Shut. Opened once more with a squeak.

I held back my amusement as she slowly walked up to me.

"You're...you're..." She pointed at me. "Octavia Ricci! I can't believe you're here." Another squeak emerged from her.

"Nice to meet you." I offered a smile and my hand.

She squeezed it, pumping it up and down. "Do you have a kid here?"

"No. I'm just here to see how the classes go." I shifted my fingers, and she finally released my hand.

"I'm Shawna."

"Hi, Shawna."

She stared at my knee brace. "Are you going to dance again?"

"I hope so." I shrugged. "Too early to know yet." And for once, the thought didn't paralyze me.

Her brow furrowed. "I'll be praying for you."

"Thank you." It never amazed me how sweet people could be. "I really appreciate that."

Her head bobbed. "No problem. Are you *really* going to watch our class?"

"I am. I can't wait to see how you guys do."

Shawna straightened. "We'll make you proud. Madame Giselle is an excellent teacher."

"I believe it. She's an excellent dancer."

"So are you." Shawna bowed and headed for the barre.

I counted eight girls now, all in various positions of warmup. Some were swinging their arms in circles. Others were doing simple stretches or jumping jacks.

Giselle walked in moments later, eyes roving over each girl. She spared me no glance as she started the class and walked them through a *rond de jambe par terre.* As the girls swept their right legs around, holding themselves erect, arms mirroring the movement, Giselle assessed each motion to ensure it was being executed properly.

I watched, mulling over the ramifications this change could effect in my life. If I retired from the company and became a teacher, I'd remain on the sidelines. My studio time would be devoted to others. Molding others into the best version of themselves. Sure, I could put on productions, but I'd no longer be the center focus. Could I live a life solely backstage? Give up dancing for an audience?

I had to admit, I'd had a good career. Achieved the status of principal ballerina in a famed company. The only thing left for me to do was to think of my life *after* ballet. To let one dream go and see what the Lord had next for me.

But I wasn't sure when I'd be able to lead a class. My leg was still healing, and my surgeon certainly hadn't cleared me for full activity. Of course, if one of the girls in Giselle's classes was really adept, I could have her execute a move to demonstrate then have the others mimic her form. Until I was in tip-top shape to do it myself, at least.

My shoulders relaxed. The idea had merit. And maybe, just maybe, this studio was a new dream, a new direction God was giving me. One where I could still leave my mark on the ballet world and keep close to the art I loved so much.

Now if only I could figure out the nuances of my social life.

I had thought of my parents' conversation every day since that heart-to-heart moment we'd shared. My father had left for Tuscany a day later, promising to keep in better touch. My mom had returned to her home a week later, once I was more mobile.

I'd only texted Noah a time or two since seeing him at the hospital. Asked him how his day was going. Surface topics. I had the feeling the ball was firmly in my court, and that thought put my nerves on edge. What should I do next? How did I move from the friend zone to more?

Was I ready?

Could I lay down my fears and embrace the freedom of living for God only? I'd been trying to please those around me for so long, I wasn't sure how to flip the switch. But I wanted to. Especially if Noah was on the other side of that.

Lord, please show me how to live for You. To glorify You. In thought, in deed, and in love.

My breath hitched, and I blinked. Noah deserved the best of me, because I wanted to be with him. And I needed him to know that I didn't care what others thought. That I was all in and ready to see what could happen between us.

I blew out a breath, letting the idea settle in my brain. Checking my emotions to ensure they weren't freaking out. All I felt was peace.

Thank You.

But how did I tell him? Did I send a text? Ask him to meet me?

I opened my group text.

O: I WANT TO BE WITH NOAH. HOW DO I TELL HIM?

H: YAY! IT'S ABOUT TIME.

T: BEST DECISION YOU'VE MADE YET.

I chuckled.

O: WELL?

H: NOT BY TEXT.

T: SO AGREE. WHAT ABOUT A BIG GESTURE LIKE IN THE MOVIES?

O: SO I SHOULD HIRE A BAND TO SERENADE HIM?

H: I COULD GRAB MY GUITAR AND BE YOUR BACK UP!

I bit back a laugh. Too bad I couldn't sing. I texted as much.

T: SINCE HE'S BEEN WRITING YOU, MAYBE YOU SHOULD WRITE BACK?

My nose wrinkled.

O: THAT'S NOT BIG ENOUGH.

H: HANG OUTSIDE HIS WINDOW AND PLAY HIS FAVORITE SONG.

T: OR YOU COULD TAKE HIM TO

A PARK AND ROLL DOWN A HILL

TO EXPRESS YOUR SORROW.

I giggled, then froze as the girls all turned to look at me. "Sorry." I slid my phone back into my purse and returned my attention to the class.

❧ 33 ❧

I STOOD OUTSIDE NOAH'S DOOR DRESSED IN MY FAVORITE OUTFIT. A cute lavender dress with black tights stuffed in ballet flats. The shoes weren't my favorite, but I still wasn't ready for heels.

Now all I had to do was knock on his apartment door. It was seven in the evening, so I figured he had to be home. And if not, then I was prepared to wait in the lobby downstairs so I didn't appear like a stalker outside his door. But first, I had to get up the guts to knock.

"How long do you plan on standing there?"

I froze at Noah's amused question. Slowly, I turned to face him. He leaned against the opposite wall, hands in pockets as he studied me.

My breath hitched. "Noah," I whispered.

"Hi, Octavia."

"Hi." I bit my lip as my eyes roamed his face. Cataloging every feature. Imprinting his puppy dog eyes, slender nose, and kissable lips to memory. His hair had been trimmed and, for once, wasn't messy. I kind of missed the mussed style.

"What are you doing here?"

I swallowed. This was it. Time for me to say my rehearsed speech. "I had to see you."

He nodded slowly. "Okay. Would you like to come in?"

"Yes, please." I moved aside, and he walked forward, key extended.

I wanted to wrap my arms around him and never let go. To beg for his forgiveness and ask that he excuse my short-sightedness. But I needed to stay on script. I should have written my words down so I wouldn't forget.

Noah opened the door, gesturing for me to follow. I peeked into his apartment, noting the wide-open floor plan. His place was decorated in muted browns and rusty reds. It had his personality written all over it. And seemed perfectly cozy.

I turned to him. "Your place is wonderful."

"Thank you." He swallowed a few times as if gathering his thoughts. "Do you want something to drink?"

"Water?"

"Sure thing." He walked to the kitchen and grabbed a bottle. "Here you go."

"Thank you." I twisted the top and guzzled the contents. My nerves had parched my throat. Besides, drinking the water gave me something to do. Something to focus on other than why I'd come. I handed him the empty water bottle.

His brows lifted in bemusement. "How long were you waiting in the hallway?"

"Five minutes."

"Thirsty work, huh?"

I giggled. "Nerve wracking."

He placed the container on the counter. "Why don't you tell me what's up."

"Well…you see…" I inhaled, trying to find the words. "I miss you." I looked into his eyes. Loving the green. Loving how steadily they gazed back at me. "I miss seeing you three times a week. I miss talking to you on the phone. I miss going out with you and having fun, discovering who you are and who I am with you."

I gulped, trying to remember all I'd wanted to say. "I'm sorry, Noah. Sorry that I let others dictate my life. Dictate my fears. Dictate what I wanted. And even more, I'm sorry for hurting you. For stepping away instead of working through the problem with you. You've been so willing to jump into a relationship with me. I hate that I hurt you by blocking you and not talking to you and then dragging my feet." I took a step forward.

"You're the best for me and I want nothing more than to be the best for you. If you'll give me another chance, I promise not to take it for granted. Or you. I promise that I'll be following God and not what some internet troll says. I promise to let love have its perfect work." I paused, my pulse pounding so hard that my head spun from the exertion of my heart.

I gripped the sides of my dress, wanting to wrap my arms around Noah instead. But he hadn't said anything. Hadn't even blinked since I started talking, and I didn't know if that was a good thing or what.

"Are you done?" he asked.

"Yes," I whispered. I bit the inside of my lip to keep from demanding a response from him.

"Good." Noah closed the gap between us and pressed his lips to mine.

A sigh escaped as he threaded his fingers through my hair and cradled my neck. I quickly wrapped my arms around his waist and clung to him as he deepened the kiss. Electricity coursed through me at his touch.

Noah broke off the kiss, placing a softer one on my left cheek then my right. "I was going to give you another week before I came over begging for a second chance."

I grinned, pulling back to look into his eyes. "Really?"

"Really." He brushed my hair from my face. "I hoped all

the texting meant you were thinking about me, about us. But part of me was afraid to hope. Until you showed up, that is."

"I'm glad I came. Holiday suggested I serenade you."

He laughed. "Can you sing?"

"Not at all. I wanted to woo you, not chase you away."

"I'm not going anywhere." He kissed my forehead.

"I'm not either. I'm so sorry."

"All's forgiven." He brushed his lips against mine. "I don't hold grudges."

"Thank goodness." I kissed him, squeezing my arms around him once more before letting go. I took a step back, needing some air. "I think being in here might be dangerous to my virtue."

Noah's face flushed red. "Right. Sorry." He stepped back, sliding his hands once more into his pockets. "Should we go out? Grab some dinner?"

"That sounds good. What are you in the mood for?"

Desire darkened his eyes, and heat filled my face. "Wrong word choice," I squeaked.

Noah chuckled, rubbing his chin. "Let's get out of here." He grabbed his keys and my hand and tugged me out into the hallway. "Chinese?"

"Sounds great."

He slid his fingers through mine, and we strolled toward the elevator. I felt so lighthearted. So carefree. If I could, I'd do a grand jeté. I giggled and squeezed his hand, thankful that telling him how I felt had ended well.

The doors slid open, and Noah's mom walked out.

My stomach dropped. How had I forgotten her and the conversation we'd had? But no, I couldn't let her chip at my resolve. I straightened my shoulders and met her stare head on.

"Hello, Mrs. Wright."

"Octavia." She dipped her head then eyed Noah. "Son."

"Mom. I didn't know you were coming over." He held up our hands. "We were just headed to grab some dinner."

"Oh."

He lowered our hands, his thumb caressing the back of mine, as if reassuring me all would be well. I tried to maintain a pleasant expression on my face as I waited to see what she'd do.

"You two are together?" Her voice shook.

With surprise or anger? "We are," I said.

"Are you sure about this?" She pointed a finger, waving it back and forth.

"I am." I looked up at Noah and smiled.

"So am I." He bent, placing a kiss on my forehead.

Tension eased out of my body at his calm acceptance. I squeezed his hand and leaned against him.

"Well. Then I won't hold you up."

I reverted my gaze back to his mom. Did that have a double meaning or was I reading more into her words than she meant?

Right now, her liking me didn't matter. All I cared about was Noah and his forgiveness.

"I'll talk to you later," Noah said as we all got into the elevator.

"Sure." Mrs. Wright speared me with a look. "I hope you have a good evening."

I nodded and whispered a thank you. Apology or not, I'd treat her words as an olive branch. If she knew we were serious, maybe she would support us instead of hindering us.

"You ready?" Noah asked, breaking through my musings.

"Ready." I smiled.

34

My phone rang and an incoming request to video call flashed at me. I swiped the icon and smiled at Bianca.

"Buongiorno, Bee. How are you?"

"I am chilly. There is a lot of wind today." Her eyes squinted at the camera, the sun's glare flitting across her face. "How is your knee?"

"Better. Stronger." So far, the second surgery seemed to have been more successful.

"Bene, bene. And Noah?"

I couldn't stop the smile that spread across my face. "He's wonderful."

"Oh good. I am so glad you gave him a chance."

Bianca and I had texted a lot more since my holiday trip. She was true to her word and FaceTimed me at least once a month.

"I am too. How's your hubby?"

"*Perfetto.* I think I may be…" Her voice trailed as her lips curved upward.

"You're pregnant?"

Bianca's head nodded with excitement, and a little squeal fell from her lips.

"Congratulations! I'm so happy for you."

"You are the second to know."

I placed a hand on my heart. "Really? Who else did you tell?"

"My husband of course."

"Of course," I repeated, a silly grin on my face. "This is the best news ever."

"You'll be next before we know it."

I giggled. "I'm enjoying dating."

"Are you still going to Giselle's studio?"

I nodded. "She's been showing me the ropes. I even had a meeting with her accountant."

"So do you think you will buy her out?"

"What do you think?" I bit my lip.

I'd been praying for wisdom and peace in a decision. Giselle wanted to start the transitioning process, but only if I wanted to buy it. I had to give her a decision or she would advertise her studio was up for sale.

"If you buy it and then dance professionally once more, can you have both?"

My mouth dropped. "That's a good question."

"I come up with them every now and then." She winked.

Or it could have been a squint from the sun again. I leaned against my headboard. "Pray for me, Bee. I really hope I can make the right choice."

"You will. Riccis do not make bad decisions."

I laughed. That sounded like something Babbo would say. I mentioned that to Bianca.

She agreed wholeheartedly. "Have you talked to him lately?"

"Yesterday. He got the invitation for Holiday's wedding."

"It was so nice of her to invite us. I had to say no. I don't want to travel pregnant. Do you think that is foolish?"

"Not at all. Do what you feel is comfortable." I wanted to

pinch myself, that I was having this type of conversation with my sister.

For so many years Bianca had felt like the relative you know you're related to but that was it. Now we had a connection. Not one as strong as the relationship I had with Holiday and Tori, but I had faith we would get there one day.

We continued to talk and catch up on our lives, and then we ended the call.

I stared up at the ceiling, as if I could see right into the heavens, and smiled. Once I got out of my own way, the doors God opened for me seemed endless. There was no limit to His blessings, only the constraints of my mind.

My future was in His hands, and that was the best place for it to be. Sure, I had days where sorrow greeted me, knowing I wasn't hundred percent with my health, but Noah encouraged me and kept me active.

If I didn't return to professional dancing, it wouldn't be for lack of trying. It would be God's will, and I was accepting that more and more every day.

EPILOGUE

THE CLASS WAS READY FOR THEIR PERFORMANCE. MY HEART thudded as I waited for the music to start and the girls to begin their routines. My nerves were tighter than if I were the one on stage dancing in front of the crowd. Who knew taking over Giselle's studio and putting on my first production would have me wishing for a paper bag to breathe into?

I'd made the decision to retire in April after spending my free time at Giselle's studio. The company had given me a wonderful send off and offered to recommend the studio to interested parties.

In May, I'd signed the paperwork purchasing the studio from Giselle. Thankfully, my lawyers had already done all the necessary legwork. I even had scholarships in place for minority groups and low-income families who wanted to send their children to a reputable studio without having to decide between pointe shoes or food.

My leg was almost back to full strength, although it still objected when I did certain moves. I doubted I would ever dance without feeling the aches and pains of my injury, but I could give my all to my students and help further their futures in the art.

Now, the opening strains of Act I of Prokofiev's *Romeo and Juliet* ushered my ballerinas onto the stage. I smiled, anticipation for the day finally breaking through, even though my mental to-do list spun through my head as I made sure everyone was prepped and ready for their turn on stage.

I'd thought being behind the stage in a supervisory role would make the distance between me and the dance I loved so much widen, but I'd been wrong. There was nothing like seeing one's dancers move in harmony after hours and hours of hard work. Their efforts were on full display as they twirled around in their costumes.

Every student from every class I taught at the studio had a role in the production, from the youngest ballerinas to the oldest. I listened as the audience clapped in appropriate spots, then signaled for the next group to go out.

I kept this up until the final scene played before my eyes and the audience stood with a roar of applause. I'd done it. Put on my first production as a ballet teacher and a retired dancer.

I stepped on stage to thank the patrons and the parents. If it weren't for their dedication to bringing their children to the studio, today wouldn't have happened. I paused for a moment, the microphone feeling heavy in my hands as I choked back emotion.

God had given me so much once I'd stopped clinging so tightly to my ideals. My dreams. My wants. He'd blessed me with a new way of life, and I couldn't figure out how to say those words.

A murmur went through the crowd, and I looked up from my shoes to see what the problem was. My mouth dropped as Noah climbed up the stage steps and stood before me, taking the mic out of my hand.

"I think what Ms. Ricci is trying to say is *thank you*." He looked at me. "Am I right?"

I nodded, and the audience laughed.

"For those of you wondering why I stole the mic from her, I had some things I wanted to say to Octavia, and I thought what better way to make a fool of myself than at the end of one of her performances? So here goes."

He turned his back on the audience and dropped to one knee.

Mamma Mia! Was he doing what I thought he was doing? I barely registered my hands wringing together as my pulse thundered in my ears.

"Octavia Ricci, knowing you has enriched my life in unspeakable ways. You brighten my life, and every day we're together I thank God. And now I kneel before you, praying you will say yes to a very important question."

I smiled.

"Octavia Ricci, will you marry me?"

"Yes," I shouted.

The audience applauded as Noah wrapped his arms around me and gave me the sweetest kiss I'd ever received. When he pulled back, he took a ring out of his pocket and slid it onto my finger.

I stared down at the simple round diamond gleaming in the gold band. Perfetto. "I love it," I whispered. I peered up into his eyes. "I love you."

"*Te amo, mio cuore.*"

"You are my heart too," I whispered against his lips before sealing my declaration with a kiss.

I CURVED MY ARMS AROUND NOAH'S NECK, RUNNING MY FINGERS through the hair at the nape. He nuzzled the spot below my ear as he swayed us around the dance floor.

Holiday's wedding had been pure perfection, but I found myself enjoying the reception much more. Being in Noah's arms without a care in the world was so freeing.

The world had gotten used to seeing us together, although the racist comments hadn't stopped. Unfortunately, they'd ramped up a little after our engagement hit the newsstands. But I'd wised up and no longer read the remarks or allowed them to gain a foothold in my mind or spirit. Instead, I thought about the love I had for this man and the love he had for me.

I knew without a doubt we'd one day be dancing at our own wedding. We hadn't decided on a date yet. My father wanted to make sure he could attend, so we were waiting for him to finalize his work schedule before setting a date.

And wonder of wonders, Mrs. Wright was looking forward to our nuptials. I doubted we'd ever be besties, but we had established a friendly relationship.

"Where are they honeymooning again?" Noah asked, straightening up and peering down into my eyes.

"Australia."

"Wow. That's pretty far away."

Holiday really wanted to experience an Australian winter. Frankly, I would have picked someplace warmer. "But they'll be happy."

"I can't believe they're going to live in the townhouse. It'll be weird not picking you up there anymore."

"It made sense for me to move out. I mean, they both want kids, and the place has plenty of room to grow a family." Besides, I wouldn't be living alone for much longer.

"True. But don't you get lonely?"

"Sometimes. I definitely haven't gotten used to the silence. It's so unnerving I spend time listening to the TV or playing music in the background."

"Maybe you should get a pet."

"No, thanks."

Noah's eyes widened. "How have we not discussed this? Do you not like dogs?"

I grinned. "Dogs are adorable."

"And cats?"

"I'll pass."

"Okay, we're still compatible." His arm tightened around me as he swung me around the floor.

I giggled at the movement. God had given me so much when he brought this man into my life.

"You look really happy today," Noah murmured. He placed a kiss on my cheek.

"I'm always happy in your arms. It's my favorite place."

"Man, I love you," Noah growled, squeezing me closer.

"And I love you." And oh, how I relished each time he told me.

"Octavia?" He whispered my name in my ear.

"Hmm?"

"I think we should pick a wedding date soon. I'm tired of saying good night to you and going back to my place." He pulled back, his green eyes searching mine. "What do you say we make this a short engagement?"

"We've only been engaged a month. How short are you thinking?"

"I'm not doing anything next month. You?"

I giggled, lightly cuffing his arm. "You're hilarious."

"Uh…" He cleared his throat. "I'm actually serious."

I halted. "Wait. Really?"

He nodded. "I love you. I want to be with you. Same house. Or apartment." He shrugged a shoulder. "You understand what I'm trying to say, despite my nerves, right?"

"I do." I paused.

"So July? August at the latest." He leaned his forehead against mine. "I spoke to your dad. He said either month works for him."

"Then yes. Let's set a date."

"Thank you, Lord!" he mouthed, looking up at the ceiling before twirling me around.

I leaned my head against his chest as he continued navigating us around the dance floor. My gaze locked onto Tori. Fox had her in an embrace, his hands spanning her swollen belly. My heart felt near to bursting.

God was good, and today I would count my blessings while dancing praises to Him.

ACKNOWLEDGMENTS

I can't believe the series is over. I had such a great time writing these books and so much help. I'd like to first thank my critique partners for being not just my first set of eyes but friends. Andrea Boyd, Jaycee Weaver, and Sarah Monzon, you are the best!

Writing Octavia's story couldn't be done without help from two important people. First up, ballerina extraordinaire Grace Hackett. Thank you so much for helping me with all the ballet terminology, the scenes, and for reading it as a beta reader. You rock!

Second, many thanks to Jessi Shull for giving me insight to ACL surgery and how that impacted your dancing. I so appreciate you answering my many questions. (And any fault in ballet terminology or ACL recovery process is entirely my own.)

I also have to give a huge thanks to my beta readers. Ashley Espie, Marylin Furumasu, Carrie Schmidt, and Vicky Sluiter. Your feedback was invaluable, and I can't thank you enough for taking the time to read the entire series for me on such a tight deadline. I so appreciate you ladies!

And of course I can't forget my awesome editor Katie

Donovan. Thank you so much for all of your hard work. You had so much going on and Octavia required extra work. Thank you for being such a blessing!

Last but not least, I'd like to thank my husband and kids for putting up with vacant stares as I write, and you try and ask me questions. I love you much!

ABOUT THE AUTHOR

Toni Shiloh is a wife, mom, and multi-published Christian contemporary romance author. She writes to bring her Savior glory and to learn more about His grace.

Her novel, *Grace Restored*, was a 2019 Holt Medallion finalist and *Risking Love* is a 2020 Selah Award finalist. She is a member of the American Christian Fiction Writers (ACFW) and president of the Virginia Chapter.

You can find her on her website at http://tonishiloh.com. Signup for her Book News newsletter at http://eepurl.com/gcMfqT.

MORE BOOKS BY TONI SHILOH

The Maple Run Series
Buying Love
Finding Love
Enduring Love
Risking Love

Faith & Fortune Series
The Trouble With Love
The Truth About Fame

CPSIA information can be obtained
at www.ICGtesting.com
Printed in the USA
LVHW020818271021
701667LV00004BA/547